WILL RED GET THE BOOT?

Veronica jumped to the ground, flinging her reins angrily at Red O'Malley.

"Did you hear me? Garnet behaved horribly, and it was your fault. You intentionally put this harsh bit on her to make her uncomfortable. Obviously a horse this sensitive doesn't need a bit like this! Poor thing, she was so nervous and scared, she could barely walk."

Red sighed. In a quiet, polite voice, he reminded Veronica that she had specifically asked him to switch Garnet's usual bit for the more severe one.

"I did *not!*" Veronica exclaimed. She eyed Red menacingly. "How dare you say that! How dare you talk back to me! Or have you forgotten who's the paying customer around here and who's the stable hand? I guess I'll just have to have my father talk to Max about you." With that final threat, Veronica stormed off into the barn.

THE SADDLE CLUB

STABLE GROOM

BONNIE BRYANT

A SKYLARK BOOK
NEW YORK • TORONTO • LONDON • SYDNEY • AUCKLAND

RL 5, 009–012

STABLE GROOM
A Skylark Book / July 1995

Skylark Books is a registered trademark of Bantam Books,
a division of Bantam Doubleday Dell Publishing Group, Inc.
Registered in U.S. Patent and Trademark Office and elsewhere.

"The Saddle Club" is a trademark of Bonnie Bryant Hiller.
The Saddle Club design/logo, which consists of
a riding crop and a riding hat, is a
trademark of Bantam Books.

ISBN 0-553-48263-7

Published simultaneously in the United States and Canada

Bantam Books are published by Bantam Books, a division of Bantam Doubleday Dell Publishing Group, Inc. Its trademark, consisting of the words
"Bantam Books" and the portrayal of a rooster, is Registered in U.S. Patent
and Trademark Office and in other countries. Marca Registrada. Bantam
Books, 1540 Broadway, New York, New York 10036.

PRINTED IN THE UNITED STATES OF AMERICA
OPM   0 9 8 7 6 5 4 3 2 1

*I would like to express my special thanks
to Caitlin Macy
for her help in the writing of this book.*

STEVIE LAKE PAUSED to catch her breath. She had been running all the way from home to Pine Hollow Stables to make it in time for her Pony Club meeting. Unfortunately, a glance at her watch revealed that she was a good five minutes late already. Stevie sighed. To the average person, five minutes might not seem like very long. But to Max Regnery, the owner of Pine Hollow and the instructor of the local Pony Club, Horse Wise, five minutes might as well be five years. Once you were late, you were late. Period. Prepared for the worst, Stevie hurried to Max's office, where Horse Wise was meeting.

Bursting through the office door, full of apologies

1

and explanations, she was dismayed to find the room empty. That was even worse. That meant the other Pony Clubbers had already moved out to the stables to discuss the topic of the day's unmounted meeting.

"Stupid closet!" Stevie muttered. Her closet was the reason she was late. Just as she had been about to leave, it had erupted in a mountain of clothes, shoes, schoolbooks, riding equipment, and stuffed animals. The noise had attracted the attention of Stevie's mother. Mrs. Lake, a stickler for housework, had taken one look at the wall-to-wall clutter and said, "Of course, I don't need to remind you that you'll clean this up before you go to Pony Club, dear."

There had been no getting around her mother, and there would be no getting around Max. Gritting her teeth, Stevie turned to go find the group. She knew she had better rush in order not to miss any more of the meeting. However, Stevie thought, pausing for a second, she didn't have to rush *so* much that she couldn't stop to look at something that caught her eye on Max's desk.

For months there had been a pile of cruise brochures sitting on a corner of the heavy oak desk. Stevie and her two best friends, Carole Hanson and Lisa Atwood, had assumed that Max and Deborah, his fiancée, were planning to go for a cruise on their hon-

2

eymoon. But since nothing had been said about their wedding date—and the brochures had stayed put— the girls had figured it must still be a long way off. Obviously, Max and Deborah were just gathering preliminary information. But now the pile of brochures was gone, and there was only one brochure left. Taking a quick look around to make sure she was still alone, Stevie grabbed the brochure. She knew she was being nosy, but she just had to find out what was going on with Max and Deborah.

"Sail the Caribbean on the magnificent cruise ship *Ocean Pearl*!" Stevie read, glancing over the pictures of plush suites and decadent banquets. Then she inhaled sharply. The departure date of the cruise was less than a month away. That could mean only one thing: Max and Deborah were finally going to be married! Stevie was delighted with the news. The couple had had a somewhat rocky courtship—no thanks, Stevie remembered wryly, to The Saddle Club.

The Saddle Club was a group that Stevie, Lisa, and Carole had started. Its rules were simple: Members had to be crazy about horses and willing to help one another in any situation. But the situations themselves were often quite complicated. For instance, when Deborah first came to Pine Hollow, The Saddle Club had been convinced that she was unfriendly—

even cold. They hadn't realized that she was just inse-cure around horses because she didn't know much about them. They *also* hadn't realized something much more important: The reason she kept coming back to the stables was to see Max! The three girls had behaved rudely toward her. Luckily, when they figured out that Max and Deborah were in love, The Saddle Club concocted one of their famous plans and reversed all the damage they had done. Stevie smiled to herself at the memory of Max's face when he saw the Fourth of July fireworks display that they had helped Deborah think up. It had read simply, "Marry me, Max!" Stevie was the one who usually got the three of them into—and out of—mix-ups. Her sense of fun and adventure almost always overrode her com-mon sense.

Lisa and Carole weren't quite as prone to scheming as Stevie. With her straight-A average and her other interests besides riding, Lisa was just too busy. Carole, meanwhile, was so devoted to horses that she often forgot the rest of the world existed.

Stevie could hardly wait to share her discovery about the cruise with Lisa and Carole. They would be just as excited as she was about Max and Deborah. Sometimes, she thought, being late had its advan-tages.

4

Taking a final look at the date on the brochure, Stevie charged out to the barn to catch up with Horse Wise. She found the group assembled inside the grain room. At unmounted meetings Max usually chose some aspect of stable management to talk about. As Stevie approached, she could tell that today's topic was feeding. Sidling up to the group, Stevie kept her eyes down, hoping Max wouldn't notice her arrival.

"When I was in Pony Club, we didn't have mixtures like pellets and sweet feed," Max was saying, "which is why everyone fed pure oats and corn. Of course, some trainers—" He paused, mid-sentence. Stevie froze. She looked up. Max had fixed a disapproving eye on her. He let it linger for a moment while she squirmed. Then he cleared his throat and continued. "Of course, some trainers still prefer to mix their own feed, and we keep oats available . . ."

Stevie let out a sigh of relief. Strangely enough, Max hadn't given her a lecture about tardiness. She smiled to herself: It was incredible how much being about to get married could improve some people's personalities.

"So how would you know what a proper feeding schedule for your horse is? Veronica, let's start with you. How would you know what and when Garnet should be eating?"

5

Veronica diAngelo's face wrinkled into a frown. She shrugged. "I'd ask Red. That's his job, isn't it?"

The Saddle Club looked at one another, rolling their eyes. It was a typical answer for Veronica, the stable snob. The girl never cleaned a piece of tack, groomed, or, evidently, fed her own horse if she could help it. Instead, she depended on the head stable hand, Red O'Malley, to do all her work for her. It worked fine at horse shows, where she showed up with Garnet looking immaculate every time, and the judges never knew any better. But in Pony Club, where horsemanship and stable management counted as much as riding ability, her attitude made her look ridiculous and kept her from passing higher ratings.

Max clenched his teeth, visibly trying to control his annoyance. "Never mind," he said curtly. "Why doesn't someone else answer the question."

Stevie, Lisa, and Carole were in shock. It was one thing for Stevie to get away with being ten minutes late. But it was quite another for Max not to reprimand Veronica for such a typically rude answer. Even his upcoming wedding couldn't have affected him that much.

In response, Lisa whispered, "He's trying not to lose his temper in front of the guest." She pointed to an attractive young woman leaning on the grain bins behind Max whom Stevie hadn't noticed. Before she could whisper back to Lisa and ask who the woman was, Max's words broke through her thoughts.

"And now I'd like Denise to tell you about planning an overall diet for your horse," Max said. He turned and gestured to the woman. "But first, Denise, why don't I officially introduce you to Horse Wise? Everyone, meet Denise McCaskill. She knows all about Pony Club, since she is an A-rated member. She's also a certified riding counselor and instructor" —Max waved his hands to quiet the excited chatter that had broken out—"and Denise can fill you in on the rest."

Denise smiled invitingly at the group. "It might take me a few days to learn all of your names, so please bear with me. Let's see . . . as Max said, I do have my 'A.' I grew up in the Midwest, and my home club is Ridgeway Pony Club, outside of Indianapolis, Indiana. Right now I'm in college in Virginia, though, so that's why I'm here. I'm on a scholarship to major in equine studies. I met Max when he was giving a lecture to us about owning and operating a farm like Pine Hollow. So, I guess that's about it. We can start the discussion."

Stevie elbowed Carole and Lisa, whom she was standing between, and gave them the thumbs-up sign.

"She seems neat, huh?" she whispered. Carole and Lisa nodded eagerly.

Denise proved herself to be both knowledgeable and fun. She was petite with dark brown eyes and dark brown hair that she kept in a long braid down her back. Her tanned face and sunburnt nose showed how much time she spent outdoors. She smiled a lot, and when she spoke she sounded confident yet modest. Everyone looked impressed, listening intently. After a few minutes Denise paused to pose a question to the group. "Can anyone tell me what 'roughage' is?" she asked.

Stevie spoke up. "Yeah, it's when my brothers and I get in a fight and beat each other up," she joked. Then she bit her tongue. She always forgot that newcomers who weren't used to her sense of humor might not find her jokes funny. She grimaced as Max frowned at her, shaking his head. But to her relief, Denise started to laugh.

"That's one of the best wrong answers I've heard," she said. "And as the only girl in a family of five children, I know all about that kind of roughage. But seriously, any other guesses?"

Carole's hand went up. "Roughage is the bulk of a horse's diet, usually grass and hay." Carole could almost always be counted on to know the right answer when it came to horse care. She had been riding since she was very little and loved every aspect of the sport. Her only dilemma was what kind of a horsey job she would have when she grew up—trainer, professional rider, or vet. Once in a while she even thought about being a blacksmith!

"Exactly," said Denise. "I like to think of roughage as the equine equivalent of salad." Her eyes twinkled as she added, "Only horses seem to be much better about eating hay than we are about eating salad. Now, who can tell me some kinds of hay and how to best store and feed it?"

The discussion went on for almost a half hour, with Max and Denise alternating who spoke and asked questions. Stevie tried to concentrate, but she could hardly pay attention, she was so excited about her find in Max's office. She kept staring at Max to see if she could notice a difference in him now that he knew the actual date of his wedding. Luckily, a lot of other people volunteered to answer questions, so she wasn't caught off guard. After what seemed like an interminable period of time, Max wrapped up the talk, reminding everyone to study the sections on feeding in the Pony Club manual before the next unmounted meeting.

As soon as Max dismissed them, a number of Pony

Clubbers, including Lisa and Carole, swarmed around Denise. Stevie sighed; the news would have to wait still longer. Denise happily answered questions about getting her "A" and majoring in equine studies. Finally, she told everyone that human nutrition was just as important as equine, and if she didn't eat lunch soon, she was going to faint from hunger. Everyone scattered to get their brown bags. Stevie, Lisa, and Carole agreed to meet outside on the knoll overlooking Pine Hollow, their traditional lunch spot.

Practically bursting with her discovery, Stevie charged out, telling her friends to hurry and join her. When they were all sitting down, Lisa told Stevie that *she* had just one question.

"What's that?" Stevie asked, impatient to share her news.

"Where's your lunch?" Lisa inquired.

Stevie looked around distractedly. In all her excitement she had forgotten to bring it out. Come to think of it, she had no idea where she had put it.

Carole and Lisa began to giggle. "You look like a dog who's lost its bone," Carole said.

"This must be pretty important if *you're* forgetting about eating," said Lisa. Usually Stevie took great enjoyment in the lunch break.

Stevie looked at her two friends disparagingly.

10

"Sometimes there are more important things to think about than eating," she said. Then it hit her where she must have left her lunch bag. The only place she had stopped had been Max's office. She had to go rescue it before it got eaten or thrown out. The news would have to wait still longer. "Don't move," she told Lisa and Carole, tearing off to the office.

"Where else would we go?" Carole called after her, shaking her head. They were used to Stevie's temporary periods of insanity, but enduring them could still be rather trying.

When Stevie got to the office, she could hear Max speaking on the telephone. The door was open, and she went in to grab her lunch off the desk, where it was sitting. Max nodded at her but kept talking. As Stevie left, his words floated up to her ears. "Right. So I'd like to go ahead and book the cruise," he said.

Stevie paused for a millisecond, grinning wildly to herself. Then she sprinted back, elated. Talk about hearing it from the horse's mouth!

SETTLING HERSELF ON the knoll between her two friends, Stevie poured out the news. "Max and Deborah are probably definitely getting married on the twenty-seventh because their cruise leaves Miami on the twenty-eighth," she explained breathlessly. "I saw the brochure on Max's desk—all the other ones were gone. And then just now I heard him say he wanted to book the cruise. Just think: In less than a month there will be a Mrs. Max Regnery III!"

The announcement had the effect on Lisa and Carole that Stevie had suspected it would. They clapped their hands together excitedly.

"That's fantastic. I'm so happy for Max—and Deborah," Carole said. "It seems like they've been engaged forever. And don't forget, we had a material part in getting them together," she added dreamily.

"Yeah, right after we had a material part in nearly breaking them up," Lisa remarked dryly.

Stevie jumped in hastily. "But let's not spend too much time remembering that part. The important thing is that they're ending up husband and wife."

"You know, that probably explains why Denise is here. If Max is going to be busy planning his wedding, he's going to need more help than just Red can give him," Carole pointed out.

"You're right," Lisa said. "And isn't Denise great?"

The three of them talked at length about how much they had liked Denise, even after just one meeting. They all thought they could learn a lot from her and have a great time with her, too.

"How old do you think she is?" Carole asked.

"Oh, I don't know. Probably around eighteen or twenty if she's in college," Lisa guessed.

"Yeah, she looks about Red's age. Why?" Stevie asked.

Carole sighed. "I was just trying to figure out how many years it would be before I could be an A-Pony Clubber, majoring in equine studies. That is, if I ever get my 'A,' " she added modestly.

" 'If' isn't a word you have to use in that context, Carole Hanson," Lisa told her. She and Stevie were fully confident that when the time came, Carole would pass her "A" with flying colors.

When they had finished eating, the three of them lay back, basking in the afternoon summer sun. "I wonder how many years it will be before we get married," Lisa murmured sleepily.

"Married?" Stevie scoffed. "Are you kidding?" Even though Stevie had a steady boyfriend, Phil Marsten, marriage was a lifetime away.

"If the groom were someone like Max, getting married would be great," Lisa insisted. "And weddings are always so much fun."

"That I'll admit. Remember Dorothy and Nigel's?" Stevie asked.

Together they reminisced about the wedding on horseback between former horse-show star Dorothy DeSoto and British Equestrian Team member Nigel Hawthorne. The Saddle Club had planned and taken part in the ceremony, which had been a horse lover's dream.

"Hey, wait a minute," Carole said, sitting up suddenly. "If Max hasn't told us when he's going to get married—even though it's a month away—that means we aren't going to be in the wedding."

14

Lisa and Stevie sat up more slowly, beginning to look worried. "It means we probably aren't even invited. You're supposed to send the invitations out six weeks ahead of time," Lisa said. Because of her socially conscious mother, Lisa knew all sorts of rules of etiquette.

"I never thought of that," Stevie said.

The three girls stared glumly at the remains of their lunches. They knew that Max and Deborah would probably want to invite lots of people their own age, but they had sort of assumed they would be included in the celebration, too. After all that had gone on, they had grown close to Deborah and felt that she was genuinely fond of them. And they had thought that Max would naturally want to invite some of his students, namely, The Saddle Club.

"It's too bad we're not invited, because we're good at weddings," Stevie said finally. "If we hadn't been there for Dorothy, who knows if she and Nigel would ever have gotten married."

"And besides, we could have helped Mrs. Reg out with the food or the punch or something," Carole said. Max's mother was a favorite among The Saddle Club. The older woman usually lost no time in getting them to help out at special Pine Hollow events.

"But they might not be having the wedding at Pine

Hollow," Lisa pointed out. "After all, sometimes the bride decides to— Hey, maybe that's it."

"What?" Carole and Stevie asked in unison.

"I was just thinking about what the bride and the groom each do at a wedding, and I remember that they usually have separate invitation lists. I'll bet Deborah's assuming that Max is inviting us, since we've been friends with him longer. But Max can be so absentminded that he's probably just forgotten to ask us."

Stevie nodded in agreement. "I'll bet you're right. He's got so much on his mind, with Pine Hollow and the honeymoon arrangements and everything, that I'm sure it just slipped his mind. So that means all we have to do is find some way to remind him."

They thought for a minute, trying to come up with a solution. "I know—how about a shower?" Lisa suggested.

Stevie gave her a withering glance. "Max seems pretty clean to me. Besides, how would that—"

Lisa cut in, laughing. "Not that kind of a shower. I meant maybe we could give him a kind of bridal shower with food and gifts and stuff."

"But he's not the bride," Stevie said, pointing out the obvious.

16

Carole grinned. "Then how about a b-r-i-d-l-e shower?" she proposed.

"Ha-ha," Stevie said.

"All right. We'll call it a 'groomal' shower for the time being," Lisa decided.

"Huh?" Stevie said.

Ever logical, Lisa explained to Stevie that showers were usually given for the bride, but in this case it seemed fair that they should have a party for the person in the wedding whom they knew best. "We could invite all of Horse Wise plus the younger riders, and Mrs. Reg, Red, Denise—maybe even Deborah."

"Right. And since it's a *groomal* shower, everyone will bring gifts of curry combs and body brushes," Stevie couldn't resist adding.

Doing her best imitation of Max when he was annoyed, Lisa raised her right eyebrow at Stevie. "Ahem. Can we get on with the planning now, Miss Lake?" she asked. She took up the notebook she always brought to unmounted meetings and began scribbling a list of things to be done. The girls had a million ideas for the shower. They all loved to plan parties, especially a party for someone like Max, who had done so much for them over the years.

At first The Saddle Club had been worried about Max's future wife, whoever she might be. They had thought she might distract Max from his horses and want him to stay at home. But they hadn't counted on a fiery redhead like Deborah Hale coming into his life. Deborah's own career as a prize-winning Washington, D.C., journalist left her little time for distracting Max. If anything, Max had to distract her. When she came to Pine Hollow, she was eager to learn as much as she could about Max's business. She threw herself whole-heartedly into life on the farm and, since the beginning of their engagement, had won the respect of everyone there. Now there was no doubt in the minds of The Saddle Club that she was the perfect match for Max.

"We have to decide on a date," Lisa reminded Carole and Stevie as they got up to go back to the stables. Lunch hour was almost over, and the unmounted meeting would resume in five minutes.

"I was thinking about that, and I think it should be on Saturday, the twentieth," Carole said. "We have a Horse Wise meeting that day, so we could plan it for right after. That way, a lot of the people we're planning to invite would be here already."

"And it's only a week before the wedding. There would be no chance of Max forgetting to invite us to something that close," Stevie said.

Lisa agreed that the date was a good one. It also

18

gave them plenty of time to get organized, which, with The Saddle Club, was always a plus.

On their way back, an inspiration came to Stevie. "Listen, if it's the custom to give the *bride* a *shower*, then maybe what we're doing is giving the *groom* a *bath*?"

Lisa and Carole laughed, but they liked the idea a lot. They decided to dub their plan the "Groom's Bath." It was such a strange name that they figured no one would be able to guess what they were up to.

"Now, who's going to bring the food?" Lisa asked, getting right to the important things as usual.

Before Stevie or Carole could respond, the conversation was interrupted by the unmistakable sound of Veronica diAngelo screeching. Veronica had skipped lunch to go riding, as she often did these days. Since she was totally uninterested in horse care, she thought unmounted meetings were a huge waste of time. So that she wouldn't "waste the entire day," as she put it, she had started riding during the break. Now she jumped to the ground, flinging her reins angrily at Red O'Malley.

"Thanks to you, I had a terrible ride!" she fairly screamed. The loud noise made Garnet prance uneasily. Red put a soothing hand on the Arabian's neck, not bothering to respond to Veronica's latest tantrum.

"Did you hear me? Garnet behaved horribly, and it was your fault. You intentionally put this harsh bit on her to make her uncomfortable. Obviously a horse this sensitive doesn't need a bit like this! Poor thing, she was so nervous and scared, she could barely walk."

Red sighed. In a quiet, polite voice, he reminded Veronica that she had specifically asked him to switch Garnet's usual bit for the more severe one.

"I did *not*!" Veronica exclaimed. She eyed Red menacingly. "How dare you say that! How dare you talk back to me! Or have you forgotten who's the paying customer around here and who's the stable hand? I guess I'll just have to have my father talk to Max about you." With that final threat, Veronica stormed off into the barn.

As usual, Red had taken a tongue-lashing from Veronica with incredible patience. Watching her go, he merely shook his head. Then he rolled up the stirrups on Garnet's saddle, loosened the girth, and began cooling off the sweaty horse.

The Saddle Club looked at one another angrily. Veronica's treatment of Red was nothing new, and lately she seemed more out of control than ever.

"The sad thing is that Red knows what she said is true: She's the paying boarder, and the diAngelos will make trouble for Max if she doesn't get her way," Carole said quietly.

"And Red doesn't want Max to have to deal with the hassle, so he just keeps quiet," Lisa noted.

The situation was depressing. Red always seemed to have to bear the brunt of Veronica's brattiness. If Max had been around, she wouldn't have dared make a scene like that because Max wouldn't hesitate to suspend her from riding. And if she launched an attack on The Saddle Club, they always found a way to get her back. But Red was stuck.

It seemed even more unfair since Red was so important to Pine Hollow. He was a real horseman and Max's right-hand man. All the things that The Saddle Club spent hours learning about in Horse Wise—conformation, feeding, saddlery, lamenesses—Red seemed to know naturally. He could answer any question about horses, he rode well, and he worked long hours uncomplainingly. He had a quiet way of doing things that seemed to reassure even the most high-strung animal. Because of his shyness, he kept a low profile around the stables. He never drew attention to his skills, and he didn't like to compete in shows, so it sometimes took months before Pine Hollow students realized how knowledgeable he was.

"If we wanted to do something really good for

someone, we'd find a way to get some relief for poor Red," Carole said reflectively.

Stevie and Lisa agreed. It seemed that they of all people ought to be able to find a way to get Veronica off Red's back. And doing that would make their own lives better because they wouldn't have to listen to her tantrums every day. But dealing with Veronica was a tricky business. The only solution for now was to think about it.

W<small>HEN THE</small> H<small>ORSE</small> W<small>ISE</small> meeting resumed, Veronica was still making a fuss. Even though Red had hardly said anything in defense of himself, the fact that he had very politely implied that she was lying about the bit had made her extremely defensive. It turned out that she had a long list of complaints about Red. She was in the midst of delivering them to Max as The Saddle Club and the other riders entered the grain room. Red, who often helped out with Max's afternoon lessons, stood by looking dismayed. He kept shifting his weight uncomfortably.

"I always see him slacking off around here," Veronica whined. She seemed to be pretending that Red wasn't in the room. "If you can't manage to get better-qualified help around here, camp won't be worth coming to."

Something she said made Lisa frown. "Camp? Isn't camp during the honeymoon?" she whispered, her eyes growing big.

Carole and Stevie looked at her in alarm. They both knew what she was thinking: In the excitement of planning the Groom's Bath, they had all forgotten about the upcoming two weeks of day camp at Pine Hollow.

Day camp was a favorite Pine Hollow summer tradition. The students came early in the morning and spent all day at the stables. They rode twice a day, had stable management meetings, and usually worked on a special exhibition for the parents, such as a drill team ride. But with Max's honeymoon scheduled to begin right in the middle of the two weeks, it would be very different.

Lisa motioned for Stevie and Carole to step outside into the aisle for a minute so they could talk. It was clear that Veronica would be complaining for at least another several minutes.

"If Veronica's upset about Red *helping* Max during camp, what's she going to say when she finds out he'll be running it?" Lisa asked.

24

"You think he'll be running it?" Stevie asked.

"Who else? Red always takes over the stables when Max goes away," Lisa replied.

"Probably Max is going to wait till the last minute to make that announcement. He'll be here the first week to get things started and then take off for the cruise," Carole guessed.

"All right. Then *nobody* breathes a word of this to Veronica—she'd probably threaten to have Red arrested," Lisa said.

Stevie put her hands on her hips, offended. "Since when do we share our secret plans with Veronica?"

Lisa smiled sweetly. "Just making sure," she said. The three of them slipped back into the grain room, where Veronica was droning on about Red's shortcomings.

Finally, Max started to protest. "If you have some specific complaints about an employee of mine, fine. But I hardly think—"

"I'm not finished," Veronica snapped. "It's clear Red doesn't know what he's doing. The bit is only one example. I've seen manure stains on Garnet's socks after Red's finished grooming her, I've caught him leading horses without their halters on. . . ."

With a look of disgust on her face, Carole turned to Stevie and Lisa. "She probably caught him patting a

horse on the wrong part of his neck," she whispered
sarcastically. She could hardly believe how totally ridiculous Veronica's complaints were—except for the
fact that they were so typical of Veronica. Everyone
knew that it was impossible to brush manure stains off
white markings. Everyone had seen Red loop his belt
around a docile broodmare's neck to guide her in at
night. Sure, if you looked up those things in a book, it
might say they were signs of bad horsemanship. But
real life with horses was different. Some things were
understandable or permissible depending upon the situation. Red was completely trustworthy.

Max folded his arms over his chest and gave Veronica a bored look. "Anything else, Veronica?" he asked,
stifling a yawn.

Veronica's eyes flashed angrily. "Yes! There is! Red
used a riding crop excessively on Garnet when he was
exercising her."

A murmur went through the group. That was a serious complaint. Red started to speak, then stopped
himself. His face was a mixture of anger and anxiety.

"Why do you think that, Veronica?" Max inquired
patiently.

"Because the next time I rode Garnet, she shied
when she saw the crop," she said triumphantly.

The Saddle Club stared at Max to see what his

26

reaction would be. In their opinion, Veronica was desperate to make an accusation that would carry some weight with Max. But if anyone was known for using a crop too much, it was Veronica herself. It was no surprise that Garnet would be crop shy around her. Making up charges against Red was just too much.

"We'll discuss this later, Veronica," Max said firmly, unable to keep the irritation out of his voice. He glanced at Denise McCaskill. The Saddle Club knew how much he hated anyone to think badly of Pine Hollow. Unfortunately, given the chance, Veronica never failed to give a terrible impression. "For now, I want you all to split up into groups to devise feeding charts for a small stable, a medium one, and a large one."

IN A MATTER of minutes, Max had the Pony Clubbers separated into three groups, headed by himself, Denise, and Red. He seemed to have concluded that keeping Veronica away from Red would provide a temporary solution. He put her on the team working with Denise. To Stevie's dismay, she was placed on that team, too. Normally, she would have jumped at the chance to work with Denise, whom they had all taken a liking to. But she was sure that Veronica would ruin everything. At the least, she would probably be incredibly rude to Denise. Stevie looked enviously at Carole and Lisa as they worked with Red.

"All right, why don't you all tell me your names again, so I can start learning them for real," Denise said when her group had gathered in a circle in one corner of the grain room. "You start," she added, pointing at Veronica.

Steve gritted her teeth. Veronica was one of the few people she knew who could turn a simple introduction into an offensive remark. Veronica smiled sweetly at Denise. "I'm Veronica diAngelo, and I'm very pleased to meet you," she said.

Stevie could hardly believe her ears. Veronica diAngelo was being friendly to an outsider? That was very strange. Usually, the only outsiders she bothered to talk to were horse-show judges. Stevie was even more shocked when Veronica continued. "We're all really excited to be working with you, Denise. I'm sure we're going to learn a lot. If there's anything I can help you with, let me know."

"Thank you, Veronica. That's very nice of you," said Denise, obviously pleased at the warm welcome.

Stevie glanced sharply at Veronica, hoping for some kind of clue as to why she was acting so unlike herself. Veronica, however, was gazing happily at Denise along with the rest of the group, as if her behavior

28

were completely normal. Come to think of it, Stevie thought, her behavior *was* completely normal—just not normal for Veronica.

When it was Stevie's turn to introduce herself, Betsy Cavanaugh had to nudge her twice before she snapped back to attention. "Oh! Sorry! I'm Stephanie —Stevie for short—Lake," she said.

"The one with all the brothers, right?" Denise said.

"Yup." Stevie nodded, pleased that Denise had remembered.

As the meeting went on, it became clear that Denise was a great teacher. She knew all the stable management techniques cold. What was more, she was patient and funny, and she kept everyone interested in the topic. She made sure that they all participated, which wasn't easy with Stevie and Veronica vying to answer all the questions first. Stevie had decided that whatever Veronica's purpose in wanting Denise to like her, she had better outdo Veronica—just in case.

After a detailed discussion about feeding a whole stable as opposed to one or two horses, Denise gave everyone pencils and paper. She told them to write their guesses as to how much hay and grain twenty horses would consume in a month and to sketch out a feed chart.

Stevie whipped off her answers and then sat puzzling. The only idea she could come up with to explain Veronica's politeness was that maybe Denise was very wealthy. Veronica always turned on the charm for rich people. Stevie looked surreptitiously at Denise. With her well-worn jeans and paddock boots and her United States Pony Club T-shirt, she certainly didn't *look* as if she had tons of money, but then again, you could never tell.

Just then Veronica looked up. "I've finished my chart, Denise, so I'll just study the Pony Club manual until everyone else is done. I always like to brush up on horsemanship," she said.

Stevie almost gagged. She noticed a couple of other riders shooting Veronica surprised looks. Nobody had seen Veronica put on this much of a show in a long time. But why? Stevie wondered again. Maybe if Denise wasn't rich, she was well connected in social circles. Veronica was certainly not above getting to know a person in the hope of meeting other people worthy of herself. Stevie took another good look at Denise, considering the idea. Finally she had to admit that seemed even less possible than her being rich. Why would somebody from Indiana be a big society person in Willow Creek, Virginia? Besides, Denise didn't act snobbish at all, the way you would expect someone like that to behave. If she was well known anywhere, Stevie was sure it was among horsey—not society—people. She certainly had the credentials to be accepted among riders anywhere.

Then suddenly it hit Stevie. Of course! Why hadn't she thought of it right away? The reason Veronica was on her best behavior was that Denise had credentials, pure and simple. With an "A" Pony Club rating, a certification as a riding counselor, and a major in equine studies at Virginia's prestigious university, Denise had won Veronica's respect. She had also won everyone else's respect. Everyone knew that getting an "A" was excellent proof of riding skill and horsemanship. The difference was that for Veronica, credentials were the *only* thing that mattered. In her opinion, if you didn't have the credentials, you couldn't possibly have the knowledge.

Red was the perfect case in point. As Max or anyone at Pine Hollow could have attested, Red O'Malley was as skilled a horseman as any "A" Pony Clubber. He was almost surely on the same level as Denise. But he had never had the time to belong to Pony Clubs, get an instructor certification, or take a university course in equine studies. There was no diploma—no piece of paper—that said Red O'Malley was a great rider and knew an incredible amount about horses, even though it was true. And he didn't have ribbons and trophies either, because he wasn't particularly interested in competitions. Therefore, to Veronica, he was just an ignorant stable hand, while Denise was someone to look up to.

Stevie let her eyes rest on Red's group for a minute. She knew from experience that his teaching style was very different from Denise's. He wouldn't ask them to write their feeding charts on paper. All his knowledge about horses was in his head, and he expected his students' to be, too. He didn't talk very much when he taught, and he didn't ask too many questions. But somehow, at the end of a session with Red, you had always learned the right answers—answers that stayed with you long after the meeting.

Of course, Veronica was always too busy ignoring Red to learn from him. With Denise, on the other hand, she was all ears. The thought annoyed Stevie. She was glad Denise wasn't going to have to deal with Veronica's outbursts, but it just didn't seem fair that Red always got the brunt of Veronica's bad temper. As Denise collected the feed charts, Stevie sighed contemplatively. Max's wedding aside, The Saddle Club just had to find a way to help Red.

When the meeting ended, most of the riders left the stables. Everyone knew that sticking around afterward usually meant that Mrs. Reg would find extra chores that needed doing. Veronica thanked Denise profusely for teaching her so much, and then disappeared. As soon as she was out of earshot, Stevie gathered The Saddle Club. She wanted to share what she'd realized during the meeting. Besides, none of them minded helping out if it meant they could all hang out at the same time.

When they were finally alone in the grain room, Stevie told Lisa and Carole about Veronica's instant adoration for Denise.

Lisa nodded. "Just what I expected. I saw a gleam in her eye the minute she heard 'A-rated Pony Clubber.' "

"It's so unfair," Stevie continued. "If Red could impress her like that somehow, Veronica would treat him ten times better." Lisa and Carole agreed. Both of them believed that Red was as knowledgeable as someone like Denise—he just didn't have the paperwork to prove it.

Mrs. Reg stuck her nose into the grain room. "I thought I heard voices in here. Listen, there are a few saddles in the tack room that could use soaping, and you know," she concluded brightly, "you can always talk and work at the same time."

The three girls followed Mrs. Reg good-naturedly into the tack room, where she pointed out the dirty tack she had noticed. Denise was inside, looking around.

"Thought I'd get a better lay of the land," she explained. "This is one of the best-organized tack rooms I've seen."

Mrs. Reg brushed off the praise, thanking Denise for instructing at the Pony Club meeting.

"My pleasure," Denise replied. "And did I hear something about some tack cleaning? Because I've always enjoyed soaping saddles."

Carole beamed. "Really? Me too! But I always thought I was the only one."

Mrs. Reg looked fondly at Carole. All of Max's students' personalities were well known to her, including Carole's passion for *anything* having to do with horses. Then she turned to Denise, saying, "That's very kind of you, but—"

Denise held up her hand to stop Mrs. Reg from protesting. "All right, then. I'm staying. Somebody hand me a sponge."

THE SADDLE CLUB was thrilled that Denise had decided to join them. Almost at once, the four of them began an animated conversation. The girls were eager to fill Denise in on the Pine Hollow traditions. They told her about the starlight trail ride at Christmastime, the Fourth of July picnic, and summer day camp.

"Of course, none of those is the most important Pine Hollow tradition," Stevie said.

Denise raised her eyebrows in curiosity. "Oh, really?"

Stevie nodded solemnly. "The most important tradition is what we're doing right now."

"Soaping saddles?" Denise asked.

"That's right: Soaping saddles, mucking out stalls, grooming horses—you name it, we do it," Stevie said with a grin. "And if you're ever standing around after a lesson like we were, Mrs. Reg will put you right to work."

Carole and Lisa nodded. "All of us pitching in around here is one of the things that makes Pine Hollow different from other stables," Carole commented.

"I'll say," Denise responded. "Everyone seems to cooperate. It's great—much nicer than places where people show up to ride their horses and then fling the reins at the stable hand."

At that, Carole, Lisa, and Stevie exchanged glances. "Actually, I shouldn't have said '*all* of us pitching in'—a few people ride but never help out in the barn," Carole said.

"Or, more precisely, one person rides and doesn't help out," Stevie couldn't resist adding.

Denise nodded sympathetically. "I have the feeling that one person just might be . . . Veronica?"

"How did you guess?" Lisa asked. The question was sincere. To them, Veronica was an obvious pain, but it usually took newcomers much longer to catch on.

"I saw that whole scene between her and Red. And I didn't like it one bit. I've seen other people butter up the instructor and then yell at the stable hands or grooms—when *I* was the groom!" Denise said. "That's how I put myself through freshman year, working in the university stables. I didn't get the scholarship until this year. So seeing people like Veronica act that way makes my blood boil."

"The best idea is to not get within thirty feet of her if you can help it, especially when there's some job she's looking for someone else to do," Stevie concluded.

"I'll remember that," Denise said. "Any other tips?"

Carole looked up from the saddle on her knees. "If you take any lessons with Max, don't let him see you fiddling around or talking—even to your horse."

"And don't be even a minute late," Stevie advised.

"Sounds like Max is pretty tough, huh? Just like my old Pony Club instructor back in Indiana. For every minute we were late, we had to scrub out a bucket," Denise recalled.

"Whatever you do, don't mention that to Max," Stevie begged. "He'll think it's a great idea, and I'll end up scrubbing buckets until I'm twenty-five!"

Denise promised not to suggest the penalty to Max, since she was so happy to be getting the lowdown from The Saddle Club. She had lots of questions for them about the history of the farm, the horses, and Max's riding career, and then she pressed them for details about themselves. Before long, Stevie had recounted a couple of her more famous practical jokes, Lisa had explained how hard it sometimes was to be a beginner, and Carole had confessed her dreams of someday rising to the highest Pony Club rating, just like Denise.

"What was it like when you got your 'A'?" Carole asked, her eyes shining.

Denise flipped her long braid back, then wrung out her sponge while she thought. She had expertly cleaned and oiled two saddles during the time the others had gotten halfway through one each. "It was one of the greatest experiences I've had," she said finally.

"Tell us about it!" Lisa urged.

"I was so nervous on the day of the test, I could barely button my coat," Denise began. "Then it got worse: I saw the horse I had to ride for the morning session. It was this little palomino—a pony. Of course, I'm small enough to ride ponies, but I considered it an insult. All the other candidates were assigned to big Thoroughbreds and warm-bloods. I remember thinking, 'I work all my life to take this test, and they put me on a pony? How am I supposed to look my best on a pony?' Then I remembered something else: Size isn't what counts. It's breeding, conformation, disposition, and training. I decided to change my attitude right away. I put a smile on my face and forced myself to keep an open mind. The minute I got on, I liked the pony. To make a long story short, the *pony* was the best *horse* at the test. It turned out he was a retired dressage star whose owner liked to support Pony Club by lending him out. So I ended up learning a lot during the test—which, after all, is the point." Denise paused as she polished a bridle's bit. "I know sometimes, when you have your tack and turnout inspections, it seems like the judges are out to get you—say, to find that one spot on your saddle that you missed cleaning. But it's really all about learning. If you forget to clean underneath the flap and you get points taken off at a rally, you probably won't forget again."

The girls looked at Denise with admiration. They knew she was being sincere when she said that the point of Pony Club was to learn. With the competitive aspect of Pony Club, it was easy to lose sight of the real aim.

"The riding counselor certification must have been a piece of cake compared to the 'A' testing," Stevie remarked.

Denise admitted that it had been a lot less nerve-racking. She took out the card that showed that she had met the standards of the certification board. It was from an organization in Indiana.

"What I want to know is how did you ever learn so much?" Carole asked.

Denise smiled. "Simple: I love horses. I spent a lot of time riding with my home club, I worked in stables in Indiana, I worked on a dude ranch. I asked questions. I rode as much as I could—my own horse and the horses of anyone else who would let me. I tried every type of riding I could. And I certainly learned a lot from the formal training I had in Pony Club, the certification program, and, now, my college courses. But none of it would have mattered a whit if I hadn't loved horses and tried to understand them. Nobody can teach you that, you know."

The girls did know. A bit shyly at first, then more openly, they told Denise about The Saddle Club. She seemed truly interested and was delighted to hear about some of their adventures and close calls. "I wish my friends and I had started a club. We certainly got into enough trouble," she said, chuckling.

When the tack-cleaning session was over, the girls felt that they had established a special bond with Denise. They had also gotten a lot of work done. Among the four of them, they had cleaned ten saddles and four bridles.

"Hey, do you want to come to TD's with us?" Stevie offered. TD's—Tastee Delight—was the local ice cream shop. "We have a lot of Saddle Club meetings there," she said. "Somehow ice cream helps us to think."

Denise thanked her but said she had other plans.

"Really? What?" Stevie asked. Carole and Lisa elbowed her simultaneously. "Oh, sorry. I guess that's kind of nosy," Stevie said. She had a habit of prying into people's lives without realizing that she was prying.

"That's okay. Anyway, it's nothing big. I'm just meeting a friend for dinner," Denise said.

They all put away the sponges and soap, placed the saddles and bridles on their racks, and dumped out the dirty water. It was nice to think of Mrs. Reg popping in later and seeing the gleaming tack. With Denise to spur them on, they had accomplished more than usual.

"So we'll see you again soon?" Lisa asked.

"Definitely," Denise promised. "I've had more fun on my first day at Pine Hollow than at any other stable." She gathered up her things and followed them out to the driveway. Red was outside, leaning over the open hood of his pickup truck. "Engine problems?" Denise inquired.

Red looked up. "Yeah. The truck hasn't been running right since the winter."

"Let me see if I can find anything," Denise volunteered.

The Saddle Club looked at one another. For some reason, it wasn't at all surprising that Denise would know a thing or two about engines. They said good-bye as she went over to join Red.

"It's nice that she's getting to know everyone so fast, isn't it?" Carole said.

"Yeah, and it's even nicer that she knows what Veronica's like without getting to know her," Stevie said. "If you know what I mean," she added impishly.

For better or for worse, they did.

5

WALKING BACK TO Stevie's house after the stop at TD's, the girls had a lot to discuss. Stevie had invited Lisa and Carole to spend the night at her house, so they had plenty of time to talk. All three of them thought Denise was a great addition to Pine Hollow. Stevie mentioned again how impressed she was with how fast the older girl had seen through Veronica's act. "It just makes me feel better knowing Veronica won't be getting any special favors while Denise is around," she explained.

Carole and Lisa nodded knowingly. Stevie had a competitive streak a mile wide when it came to Veronica. Anybody who saw Veronica as she really was—rich, rude, and spoiled—immediately won a place in Stevie's heart.

"Fortunately for us, that scene with Red really gave her away," Carole commented.

"The sad thing is that even if Denise thinks Veronica treats Red badly, she can't do anything about it. Veronica will tone down around her, the same way she acts better in front of Max. But as soon as she catches Red alone, she'll blame him for everything, as usual, and then tattle to Max—about nothing!" Lisa said. That was the problem with Veronica. She could turn her moods off and on, depending on who was around. If it was someone she wanted to impress, she was perfectly behaved. But if it was someone she didn't care about, she would scream, sulk, cry—do anything to get her way.

"Without Max there, the second half of camp is really going to be a bad week," Carole said.

Stevie nodded. "It's not that Red can't do the work, but it's going to be agonizing to have Veronica taunting him every single day."

"And Red will be working harder than ever. He'll have double duty, taking care of the stables and teaching us," Lisa said glumly.

The Saddle Club knew from experience that when Max went away, Pine Hollow was a very different place. All of a sudden the stables didn't run themselves, the way they usually seemed to.

"I say we don't go to sleep tonight until we think up a way to help Red," Stevie declared as they drew near her house.

Agreeing to stay up late wasn't exactly a problem for Lisa and Carole. Most of the time, no matter whose house they were at, the three of them talked until they were shut down by someone's parents or got so exhausted that they fell asleep midsentence.

Back at the Lakes', Stevie's brothers had constructed a fort out of tents and blankets on the front lawn. Stevie took one look at it and suggested they go in through the back door. "I know they're hiding in there, and I also know that Chad and Alex and Michael just bought new water guns," she explained. "Of course, I'd be happy to take them on, but I wouldn't want to involve you two in a messy fight, especially before dinner." She led the way around the house. As the girls reached the backyard, three darkly clad shapes jumped from behind a row of shrubs, squirting madly.

"Oh, no—the fort was a fake-out! Run for it!" Stevie cried. She, Carole, and Lisa sprinted for the back door. By the time they got into the kitchen, they were drenched.

Mrs. Lake shook her head at the sight of them. "All right, everybody upstairs to Stevie's room to change," she said. "And if you girls agree, I think the boys should set the table and do the dishes tonight."

The three girls hooted with laughter as they charged up the stairs. At the top, Stevie turned and looked down. "Really, Mother, you should try to keep better control of your *other* children," she said with a sniff. The three girls burst into laughter. Mrs. Lake shook her head, but then she broke into a chuckle, too.

"Sorry, guys," Stevie said later when the three of them had changed into dry shorts and T-shirts and were gathered on her bed.

Carole and Lisa brushed off the apology. It was a fact that coming to the Lakes' involved a certain amount of risk. You never knew what Stevie and her brothers would be at war about, but you always knew that they would be at war.

"Maybe that's what we should do to Veronica," Lisa suggested with a laugh. "Wait in hiding for her to say something rude to Red and then squirt her down."

"Too bad her temper tantrums usually occur around horses. Otherwise, I'd agree," Carole said.

Lisa nodded. "You're right—it would spook the horses. But we could kind of hide out around the sta-

46

ble and at least make a list of all the times she gets out of hand. Then we could report back to Max."

Stevie gave her a pained look. "And have The Saddle Club become a bunch of tattletales like Veronica? No way. Besides, Max knows she's horrible to Red, and unless he kicks her out of Pine Hollow, he can't do anything either."

"And that'll never happen," Lisa said matter-of-factly.

It was well known that whenever Veronica had done something outrageous, Mr. and Mrs. diAngelo would come to Pine Hollow and plead with Max to forgive her. They were important people in Willow Creek, and they donated lots of money to good causes. Offending them would be bad for business, and it wasn't something Max was eager to do.

"I wish Veronica would wake up one morning and decide to be nice to Red," Carole said wistfully.

"That would happen if Red woke up one morning with credentials like Max's or Denise's. That's the only way Veronica would respect him," Stevie said.

Lisa's eyebrows shot up. "That's a brilliant idea!" she exclaimed.

"What's a brilliant idea?" Stevie asked. She was used to stumbling upon solutions that she didn't notice until Lisa pointed them out.

47

"What you said. Red needs credentials to make Veronica respect him. So what's to stop us from getting him some credentials?"

"How can we do that?" Carole asked. "Unless he changes his mind about competing, he's never going to win trophies. I doubt he'd want to study at the university—when would he find the time? And he's too old to be a Pony Clubber, even though I'm sure he'd be an 'A.' "

"True. But he's not too old for that other certification thing that Denise has," Lisa said excitedly. "What was it again?"

"Certified Riding Counselor," Stevie replied promptly. "Equestrian Center, 101 Danvers Drive, Munroe, Indiana, 00335."

Lisa and Carole stared at her as if she were an alien from outer space.

"Is there a problem? That's the name and address of the place where Denise got her certification," Stevie said innocently. Then she cracked a smile. "I may have trouble memorizing algebra formulas and irregular French verbs, but when I'm looking at something that isn't any of my business, I never forget a comma."

Lisa and Carole congratulated her: Sometimes it helped to have a friend with a criminal mind. "So all we have to do," Lisa continued, "is write a letter to

48

the organization and tell them to send someone out here to give Red an examination. No doubt Red will pass with flying colors."

The more the girls thought about it, the more they liked the sound of Lisa's plan. Even if the certificate was just a piece of paper, it was a piece of paper that would give Red the respect he deserved from Veronica. "The whole thing is perfect," Carole said. "It will give Red the credentials he should have—"

"—and put Veronica in her place for good!" Stevie shouted gleefully.

"Girls! Dinner!" Mrs. Lake called from downstairs.

The girls promised to carry out the plan that evening. "Say, Lisa?" Stevie began as they went to wash up. "Would you mind thinking of a plan that would put my brothers in their places, too?"

AFTER GOBBLING UP their macaroni and cheese and their salads, the girls headed for Stevie's bedroom to draft a letter to the Equestrian Center. Sweeping by them, Stevie cast a haughty look at Chad, Alex, and Michael, whom Mrs. Lake had stationed at the dishwasher.

"Little did I know that their attacking us with water guns would come in so handy," she confided to

Lisa and Carole once they were upstairs. "But now we have extra time to get this letter done."

"It shouldn't take too long if we can just think up the right thing to say," Lisa said. She stuck a pen in her mouth and began chewing on it for inspiration.

"How about starting with 'To Whom It May Concern'?" Carole suggested. "I know a lot of Dad's official-type letters begin that way."

"Excellent. If it's good enough for the United States Marine Corps, it's good enough for us," Lisa said, jotting down the phrase. A colonel, Carole's father held one of the highest ranks in the Marines.

"What do you think, Stevie?" Carole asked.

Stevie looked up from the movie magazine she had pulled out from underneath her bed. "Huh? Oh, yeah, sounds great."

Lisa shot her a withering glance. "I'm sure you'll find a lot of stuff about the certification process in that article on Hollywood hunks," she said dryly.

"I'm just not good at this!" Stevie wailed. "I practically failed the business letter part of our English class. But, listen, I trust you two completely. Write whatever you want, and I'll sign it."

"Thanks a lot," Carole said sarcastically.

Stevie closed the magazine. "Okay, okay—I'll listen."

Lisa and Carole looked doubtful. "And then, when we're done," Stevie added hastily, "I'll type the letter onto my mom's computer."

"I forgot you had a computer," Lisa said. "That'll be even better. It will look very serious."

After several tries, the draft was finished. Stevie had gotten directions to Pine Hollow from an old horse-show flyer so that the examiner would be able to find it. Lisa had thrown in a lot of big words to make it sound good. She read it aloud to Stevie and Carole. " 'To Whom It May Concern: We believe that there is a person at Pine Hollow Stables of Willow Creek, Virginia, who is worthy to receive your certification as a Riding Counselor. He is skilled in all aspects of horsemanship, including riding, training, grooming, and instructing. Please consider this a formal request for you to send an official examiner to Pine Hollow to give Red O'Malley the required test so that he may gain certification as soon as possible. We enclose directions to the stables and look forward to seeing you. Sincerely yours, Stephanie Lake, Carole Hanson, and Lisa Atwood.' "

Stevie and Carole clapped enthusiastically. "The only problem is that we don't know Red's real name," Lisa pointed out.

"You mean Red isn't it?" Carole asked.

51

"I doubt it," Lisa replied. "It sounds like a nickname to me."

"We'd better put something else, then," Stevie said.

"Like what? How do we know what it's short for?" said Lisa.

Stevie thought for a minute. "I don't know—how about . . . Redford?"

The three of them looked at one another and burst out laughing. Somehow, Redford was as different from Red as a name could be. The idea of Red secretly having a stuffy, stuck-up name like Redford was hysterical.

"I'll bet Veronica would treat him better just for having that name!" Carole cried between snorts of giggles.

Stevie stood up to do her Veronica imitation. "Excuse me, Redford? Could you kindly prepare my mount for me? I shall be going hunting this afternoon." Carole and Lisa threw pillows at her.

When they had gotten control of their giggles, they went down to Mrs. Lake's study to type the letter. In the final draft Red became Redford O'Malley.

"You know, it's beginning to grow on me," Stevie said as they waited for the letter to print out. "Maybe we should see if Red answers to it."

Lisa whisked the piece of paper out of the printer.

Each of them signed her name, using Mrs. Lake's fountain pen. Then they stood back to admire their handiwork.

"If I were the Equestrian Center and I got this letter, I'd send somebody out to Pine Hollow," Carole said.

Stevie folded the letter, stuffed it into an envelope, and sealed it with a flourish. "I'll ask Mom to mail this tomorrow. So I guess now all we can do is wait for the person to show up."

"Do you think we ought to warn Red?" Carole inquired.

Lisa shook her head. "No, I don't think we should say anything. He might not love the idea. It'll be better if we wait until the examiner arrives at Pine Hollow. Then he won't be able to say no."

Although it was still early, the girls decided to change into their nightgowns and pajamas. That way they could get into their sleeping bags and talk. Stevie had discovered that her parents tended to be more lenient about her and her friends' talking until all hours of the night if they got into bed early. "I think Mom and Dad figure that we're getting rest just by being in bed," she said.

Now, with the problem of Red and Veronica at least temporarily taken care of, The Saddle Club had other things to discuss. Since it looked as if camp had a chance of working out, the three of them could hardly wait for it to start. It was always a great opportunity to work on individual riding problems, and the end-of-camp exhibition had never failed to delight both the parents and the students. Besides riding in drill teams, the camp group had performed dressage rides to music, played Pony Club games, and jumped over fences in hunt teams. Max believed it was good for his students to try all different kinds of riding. It kept them interested while sharpening their skills and giving them an appreciation for other riders' abilities.

"I wonder if Max will decide what the exhibition is going to be before he leaves, of if he'll let Red choose," Carole mused aloud. She and Lisa were spread out on Stevie's floor amid sleeping bags, blankets, pillows, and stuffed animals.

Logical as ever, Lisa guessed, "Probably they'll decide together, since they'll each be running camp for one week."

"I hope the exhibition is a re-creation of a Wild West stampede," Stevie said, not very realistically.

"Yeah, I'm sure the parents would just love to see their kids galloping madly around Pine Hollow, wouldn't they?" Carole responded dryly.

In the midst of talking about horses and the fun they were going to have at camp, the girls drifted off to sleep. "Just remember," Lisa reminded them as her head dropped to her pillow, "we have the Groom's Bath to organize before anything else."

THE FOLLOWING TUESDAY, The Saddle Club reported for their regular afternoon lesson at Pine Hollow. The class was working on relaxation for the horse and rider. Denise was back, helping Max with the instructing. While he ran the lesson, she took students down to the far end of the outdoor ring to work with them individually. Max and Denise seemed to enjoy teaching together, and all the students got attention.

Veronica showed up fifteen minutes after class started. Max spoke to her sharply. He seemed to have decided that since Denise was going to be a regular member of Pine Hollow, he could go ahead and reprimand his students in front of her. "Everyone is on summer vacation, so I don't want to hear any excuses," he said.

"But it's not my fault!" Veronica wailed. "Red didn't have Garnet ready when I got here. How can I help that?"

The Saddle Club exchanged glances. About a half hour before, all three of them had seen the chestnut Arabian waiting in her stall, fully tacked up. Veronica, however, had been nowhere in sight.

"It's not my fault that the employees at this stable can't be trusted. It's not my fault—" In the middle of her whining complaint, Veronica stopped short.

Stevie, Lisa, and Carole whipped around in their saddles to see what had stopped her. They followed her glance to the other end of the ring, where Denise stood, giving Veronica a big grin. "Hello, Veronica!" she called, waving.

Veronica smiled wanly and waved back. She looked uneasily at the rest of the group. Then, without another word of complaint against Red, she turned and began pulling down her stirrups to mount. It was clear that she had somehow put two and two together and realized that blaming the stable hand wouldn't endear her to the new instructor. By now everyone knew that Denise herself had been a stable hand and groom.

When Veronica had mounted, class resumed. Carole had just gone to work Starlight with Denise. Max had everyone else walking in a large circle on a loose rein while they did stretching exercises. First they rolled their shoulders back several times; then they took their feet out of the stirrups and rotated them slowly. They did a number of other stretches for relaxation, like toe-touching and touching their ears to their shoulders. At first some of the riders, including Lisa, were afraid to do the exercises fully.

"I don't think Prancer likes me leaning down like this," she told Max as the bay mare started to fuss. Prancer was a young Thoroughbred off the track. Lisa had been riding her in lessons and Pony Club for some time now, but she was still green, and new things tended to upset her.

"That's because she's not used to it," Max responded. "But don't worry, she will be soon: I want you all to practice warming up with these new exercises every time you ride to see how your being relaxed affects your horses."

When Carole rejoined the group, Max sent Veronica down to Denise. "Oh, Denise, I'm so happy to be working with you!" Veronica called as she trotted off.

Carole was absolutely glowing. She fell into place behind Lisa and Stevie, whispering to them that Denise was even better at teaching riding than she was at unmounted lessons.

AFTER CLASS LISA and Stevie echoed Carole's praise of Denise. "She has a way of explaining things that really makes sense," Lisa said reflectively as she hopped off Prancer.

Stevie agreed. "And no matter how great Max is, it's always good to get a fresh opinion, isn't it, Belle?" Stevie gave the sweaty chestnut's neck a good pat. "By the way, before class I spread the word about the Groom's Bath. Everyone wants to help. We're going to meet in the grain room after untacking to plan it. No one should be there at this time of day, and if Max comes in, we'll just say Denise is making us review Saturday's Horse Wise topic, okay?"

Before Lisa and Carole could respond, Veronica strode by, complaining loudly. Since Denise and Max had both gone in right after the class ended, Veronica obviously thought she now had full license to attack Red.

"You could step on it for a change, you know," she called to the stable hand. "I've been waiting for five minutes, and in case you don't realize it, I've got better things to do with my time than stand here all day."

Red, who had appeared at the rail, said nothing as

usual, but calmly and with a hint of a smile took Garnet's reins from Veronica. After lodging a few more complaints about Garnet's care, Veronica left the ring. Red scratched the horse between her ears for a minute. Then he rolled up the stirrups, loosened the girth, and, with a wave of greeting at The Saddle Club, headed back to the stable.

Lisa, Carole, and Stevie had watched the scene with a mixture of bemusement and annoyance. It was funny, in a way, that Veronica harped on everything that Red did wrong, yet never failed to expect him to do her work. Red's half-smile seemed to indicate that he felt the same way. The only consolation was that a cure was on the way. The Equestrian Center would receive the letter this week. In fact, they probably had it already.

"Stevie, you did say that you spoke to everyone about the Groom's Bath before the lesson, right?" Lisa asked.

Stevie smiled, understanding Lisa's point perfectly. "That's what I said, Lisa. So everyone who was there on time, tacking up for the lesson, knows about it."

"And the people who were late?" Carole asked, joining in.

Stevie grinned. "It's not my fault!" she wailed.

*   *   *

"ALL RIGHT! PIPE down, everybody!" Stevie announced a half hour later. Instead of just the people in their lesson, everyone who was at Pine Hollow that afternoon seemed to have shown up for the Bath meeting. "In case I didn't tell you, this is supposed to be a secret. You know? S-e-c-r-e-t, secret?" Stevie said in a stage whisper.

As soon as the din in the grain room had subsided, Stevie turned the floor over to Lisa. Lisa explained that the Groom's Bath was a party to celebrate Max's upcoming wedding to Deborah Hale and that they had decided the name "bridal shower" wouldn't do. Then she asked for volunteers to cook things, bring things, and decorate things on the twentieth.

Polly Giacomin waved her hand. "But why are you having it then? Max may not get married for another year—or ten years, for all we know."

Stevie spoke up. "Actually, Max is just about definitely getting married on the twenty-seventh of the month."

A buzz went through the crowd. Even though he had been engaged for several months, it was a different thing entirely to imagine Max married—and even stranger to think about a Mrs. Max living at Pine Hollow.

"How do you know he's getting married on the twenty-seventh?" Polly persisted.

"We have it on, ah"—Stevie paused to clear her throat—"on very good authority that this is exactly what's going to happen," she said. There was no need to explain that this "very good authority" was her snooping on Max's desk.

Coming to Stevie's rescue, Carole said firmly, "Lisa, tell us what food we need to bring."

"Right. Okay: cookies, chips, soda . . ."

In a matter of minutes Lisa had everyone signed up to bring something or to help with the preparations. Compared to some of the events that The Saddle Club had planned, the Bath was a fairly simple party. Still, it would be a nice gesture that Max and Deborah would appreciate. At the same time, it would remind them of certain people whom they had—no doubt mistakenly—left off their wedding invitation list.

After signing up to help with the Bath, the riders wandered off to tend to their horses or meet their rides home. The Saddle Club stayed behind in the grain room to go over the party plans.

"Looks to me like this 'bath' is going to be a big splash," Stevie said, attempting to keep a straight face.

Lisa and Carole groaned at her bad pun. "As long

as it's a surprise," Lisa said. "Because if it's not, it could be a complete *washout*."

"If you don't watch out, I'll wash you both out!" Carole threatened. The girls doubled over, holding their sides from laughing too much.

Without warning, the grain room door swung open. The Saddle Club immediately dropped all talk of the Bath when they saw the person standing in the doorway: It was Max's fiancée, Deborah Hale. She was dressed in breeches and boots and had her long red hair pulled back in a ponytail. When she saw The Saddle Club, she smiled. "Have you guys been eating the sweet feed again?" she kidded.

"Deborah!" the three of them fairly yelled.

"We haven't seen you in so long," Carole said, giving the woman a hug. It was great to see her, especially since she was dressed in riding clothes. When she had first come to Pine Hollow, Deborah hadn't known anything about horses. She wouldn't have known a few months ago that sweet feed is a mixture of pellets, oats, corn, and molasses, let alone been able to make a joke about it.

"I've been so busy at the newspaper that I haven't been able to get out here anywhere near as often as I would like. Poor Max usually ends up driving into D.C. to see me," Deborah explained. As a top investigative reporter for *The Washington Times*, Deborah was a busy career woman. In fact, it was through her job that she had met Max. She had been investigating a drug ring at the racetrack and had been given Max's name as someone to consult for background information on horses.

"But, judging from the clothes you're in, I'll bet you're here to ride today," Lisa said.

Deborah glanced behind her. Lowering her voice to a near whisper, she said, "Don't tell anyone, but Red has given me the best wedding present I could imagine. He knows how much I want to share Max's love of horses. To make a long story short, he offered to give me riding lessons. Things have slowed down a little at the paper, so I'll be coming out a few afternoons a week."

The girls were delighted with Deborah's news. "That's a fantastic idea!" Carole breathed. "Max will be so happy."

"Red sure knows how to pick the perfect gift," Lisa added.

"Just remember, the lessons are a surprise for Max. He doesn't even know I want to learn to ride," Deborah told them.

The Saddle Club swore to secrecy.

"How are you going to keep Max from finding out,

though?" Stevie asked. A person on a horse wasn't exactly the easiest thing to keep hidden.

"Red has it all worked out. He's going to try to teach me while Max is busy teaching other lessons, and we're going to have our lessons in the old schooling ring out back. I've told Max that I want to come out to Pine Hollow more often in the next few weeks. He assumes it's just to see him and hang out. But," Deborah added, "I was hoping that if we need to distract Max, you three might be able to concoct something."

"You mean you're kind of—well, asking us to play tricks on Max?" Stevie whispered, her eyes sparkling at the very thought.

Deborah nodded. Then, with a glance at Stevie's avid expression, she added a warning. "Of course, you wouldn't have to do anything too drastic. I do want to marry this man!" In her previous visits to Pine Hollow, Deborah had had plenty of opportunity to witness the mad confusion that The Saddle Club was capable of creating.

With a pointed look at Stevie, Carole and Lisa quickly assured her that nothing would get out of hand. "Great. Then I guess I'll see you on horseback," Deborah said excitedly. She went off to find Red, leaving the three girls to discuss this latest development.

"Now I'm more sure than ever that we were right about the wedding being on the twenty-seventh," Stevie said triumphantly. "And do you realize what this means?"

"Yes. It means that Deborah is even more in love with Max and more perfect for him than we realized," Carole said. To Carole, whose life revolved around her love for horses, learning to ride was the best present a woman could give her future, horsey husband.

"It also means that Red is even smarter and nicer than we realized," Lisa put in. "He saw that Deborah wanted to learn to ride and so he volunteered to teach her."

"Okay, okay—Red's great, Deborah's great, they're all great," Stevie said. "But the incredible thing about Deborah's riding lessons is that with the Groom's Bath and Red's certification"—she paused dramatically—"I now have three secrets to keep!"

CAROLE STEPPED BACK from Starlight to survey her grooming. She always liked to do an extra good job for mounted Horse Wise meetings, and today was no different. Starlight's bay coat shone with good health, good care, and, Carole had realized after last week's talk, good feeding.

"You've got that horse so shiny, I need my sunglasses," a cheerful voice commented. Carole turned eagerly to greet Denise, who had come up behind her and was looking at Starlight with admiration.

"Thanks! I was just thinking that it's the food Starlight eats that helps give him that healthy glow," Carole said.

"You've got that right," Denise agreed. She gave the bay gelding a pat on the shoulder. "Are you coming to the Horse Wise meeting in Max's office?"

"Oh, that's right—I was having so much fun grooming Starlight that I forgot we're supposed to meet there first," Carole said.

"Here, let me help you put him away," Denise volunteered.

"Great." Carole gathered up her brushes while Denise led Starlight back to his stall.

As they walked to Max's office, Denise observed, "You really like all aspects of horsemanship, don't you?"

Carole nodded eagerly. "I just love anything to do with horses. I don't even mind mucking out."

"That's the way I was, growing up, too," Denise said as they entered Max's office. "Still am actually," she added.

Glowing with pride, Carole went to sit with Lisa and Stevie. It wasn't as if Denise had praised her outright, but to Carole, hearing that she was like Denise was as good as any compliment Denise could give her.

Max had called everyone together to talk about the summer camp program. "It's going to be the same as it always is," he announced after quieting the group down. "Two weeks of intensive lessons."

Stevie raised her hand. She couldn't resist the opportunity to tease Max just a little. "Are you sure it's going to be *exactly* the same, Max?" she asked, elbowing Lisa and Carole.

Max looked at her oddly. "Well, every year varies slightly, and of course there's the exhibition to think of, but basically, yes. Anyway, I want to make sure we have the name of everyone who is coming to camp as well as the horse you'll be riding, so I'm sending around this sign-up sheet."

Stevie took advantage of the pause to needle Max again. "The exhibition is always the *second* week of camp, isn't it, Max?" she asked pointedly.

Max nodded, raising an eyebrow. "You know that, Stevie. It's always the last day, Saturday."

Stevie smiled knowingly. "It's too bad that *everybody* won't be able to make it this year," she said. She was surprised she hadn't gotten a rise out of Max yet. She had thought she might be able to get him to admit that he and Deborah had set a date, but so far he had kept a perfect poker face.

"Can't your parents come?" Max asked.

"Oh, yes. They'll be there, but some other people might be away," Stevie persisted suggestively.

To her disappointment, Max simply shrugged and continued the meeting. "The important announce-

69

ment I have to make is that I have a new cocounselor for the camp program. I'm sure you all can guess that it's Denise. She's going to participate in the upcoming Horse Wise meetings to get to know the riders and horses, and I'm very pleased to have her joining us."

When Max paused, the Pony Clubbers broke into spontaneous applause. Denise was fast becoming a favorite around the stables. Having her as a camp instructor would be a treat.

"What fabulous news!" Veronica gushed.

Denise stood up, motioning for everyone to stop clapping. "Thanks for the applause. You may want to withhold it when you find out how hard you'll be working during camp," she kidded.

"Do you really think she'll get Veronica to work?" Stevie murmured under her breath.

"If anyone can, it's Denise," Lisa whispered back.

"Anyway," Denise continued, "I have a few specific goals for the two weeks. One is that we all cooperate and work together to keep up the high Pine Hollow standards. I expect *everyone* to pitch in, and I won't be afraid to remind anyone who isn't . . ."

"Is it my imagination, or is she looking right at a certain someone?" Carole whispered. All three of them glanced at Veronica, who was squirming slightly in her seat.

"I'll also want to talk to each of you about your individual riding goals for the summer. So, I guess that's about it. I'm really looking forward to being at Pine Hollow full-time," Denise concluded.

When she had finished, everyone cheered again. Finally Max broke in, reminding them to bring in their signed parental permission forms.

As The Saddle Club left the office to go tack up, Stevie couldn't resist one more chance to see if Max would rise to her bait. "Camp should be really fun," she said casually, "although not as much fun as—say —taking a long sea voyage." She glanced at Max to see how he would respond.

Max looked up from the camp sign-up list, a worried expression on his face. "Stevie, I have to say, you are talking more nonsense than usual today. Is anything bothering you?" he asked.

Stevie beamed at him. "Why, no, Max, nothing's bothering *me*," she said. She slipped quickly through the door to join Carole and Lisa in the tack room, where they were gathering up their saddles, bridles, and hard hats.

"Can you believe it? He wouldn't admit a thing," Stevie whispered.

"I know," Lisa whispered back. "I didn't know he could keep a secret like that."

71

"What do you think about Denise teaching at camp?" Carole asked. "I'm so excited."

"I think it's great!" Stevie said. "It will make even less work for Max to worry about before he goes off on his romantic honeymoon cruise."

"I don't know," Lisa said worriedly. "I feel bad for Red."

"Red?" Carole repeated.

Lisa nodded. "Yes. It just shows that Max believes what Veronica's been saying about him. Why else would he hire Denise?"

"You mean you think Max doesn't trust Red to run things while he's gone? Because of Veronica?" Carole asked, horrified.

"If he did, why wouldn't he have made the usual announcement he makes—that Red is going to be his cocounselor?" Lisa said. "He didn't even mention Red."

A dark look crossed Stevie's face. "But that's totally unfair! I mean, Denise is great, but how could Max do that to Red?"

"I don't know, but I think we should have a Saddle Club meeting at lunch," Lisa said.

The girls agreed to meet at the knoll for lunch. Then they hustled to get to class on time.

*   *   *

72

"PHEW! WHAT A workout!" Carole exclaimed an hour and a half later. She sat down beside Lisa and Stevie and got out her bag lunch.

"That was fantastic," Lisa agreed. The lesson had focused on jumping, and Denise and Max had set up a stiff course that would really challenge the class. "I'm so happy that Prancer and I could keep up with the class," Lisa added. In the past it had been frustrating for her and Prancer to jump with the more experienced riders, since both of them were green over fences. But now that she felt more confident, Lisa loved to jump.

"I'll say you kept up—you were the only ones who did the in-and-out in one stride," Carole said appreciatively.

"Really?" Lisa asked.

Carole nodded. An in-and-out was a two-jump combination. Max and Denise had set the two jumps fairly far apart to challenge the horses to stretch the stride in between. But a lot of the horses had simply put in two short strides.

After a minute, Lisa asked, "Didn't you like the lesson, Stevie? Belle did so well, too." Stevie had been noticeably silent as they walked out to the knoll.

"Oh, yes—I loved it, too," Stevie replied. She paused, lost in thought. Finally she explained. "It's just that I kept thinking about what you said about Max picking Denise over Red, and I felt like I was betraying Red by enjoying the lesson." She stared glumly at her peanut butter and jelly on white.

"I know what you mean," Lisa replied. "I kept wondering why Max would start having doubts about someone who's worked for him for so long. All I could think is that maybe Max is worried that the diAngelos will try to get Red fired or something. You never know, with them. If they've been complaining about Red, too, and then Max went away, leaving him in charge, they would probably throw a fit."

"The more I think about it, the more I think maybe Max *is* beginning to look down on Red," Stevie said. "All those complaints from Veronica could be getting to him finally. He doesn't have time to go check up on Red, and Red never defends himself to Max."

"And Max is too preoccupied with his wedding to have a talk with Red," Carole added.

"At least we know that we've done the right thing by writing to the Equestrian Center," Lisa said with a sigh.

Carole looked thoughtful. "You know, it's funny. Here we thought we were doing something to help make Red's life with Veronica easier. Now it turns out that this may be a critically important thing to restore Red's reputation with Max."

On that somber note they packed up their trash and headed in. As they passed behind the stables, they caught a glimpse of a solitary rider working in the schooling ring. The red hair revealed her identity. "Red must have given up his lunch hour to teach Deborah," Lisa guessed, touched by the generosity of Red's wedding present.

"Let's go see how she's doing," Carole suggested.

Moving slowly so as not to disturb the lesson, the three of them walked over and leaned against the rail of the ring. Red had Deborah riding Delilah, the quiet palomino that a number of Max's students had learned on. She was trotting down the long side of the ring, practicing her posting.

"That's right: up, down, up, down. Think about the rhythm of the trot," Red said. His voice was full of patience and encouragement.

When Deborah turned the corner, she saw The Saddle Club and flashed them a smile. Red waved a hello, then went back to concentrating on his pupil. "Good job. You've almost got it," he said.

"I can't believe she's trotting by herself already," said Carole. "I think this is only her second lesson."

"If anyone can bring her along in time for the wedding, it's Red," Lisa said.

"I only wish Max could be here to see this," Stevie said, frowning.

"I know. It's too bad this is the one thing we can't tell him. If Max knew how Red is giving up his personal time to work with Deborah, and if he saw what a great teacher Red is, I'm sure he wouldn't have any more doubts," Carole remarked.

They watched as Red had Deborah ride through the center of the ring, changing directions—and diagonals. One of the basic things riders had to learn was diagonals. When Deborah posted, she had to make sure she rose in the saddle as Delilah's outside foreleg was coming forward. If she rose as Delilah's inside foreleg was coming forward, she would be on the wrong diagonal. Every time they switched direction in the ring, Deborah had to sit a beat, so that she'd be on the right diagonal.

When Deborah had a problem or forgot something, Red spoke to her gently. Deborah looked thrilled to be trotting. She had a huge smile on her face. It was a look The Saddle Club knew well: It came from clipping along on a horse that you liked and feeling that the two of you could do anything.

When Deborah pulled up at the end of the lesson, Stevie, Lisa, and Carole walked into the ring.

"So, you're in on the big secret, huh?" Red asked.

"We are, and we think it's the best wedding present imaginable," Carole replied.

Red smiled, then turned to Delilah to take her in.

"Oh, Red, let me do that. I'm sure you have other jobs to do. I'll cool her off and bring her in," Deborah protested.

Red shook his head. "Horses are my job, Deborah. Besides, you've got to get back to D.C. to *your* job." Before she could argue, he led Delilah out of the ring with a friendly wave for The Saddle Club.

"He is one of the most considerate people I have ever met," Deborah said when Red was out of earshot.

"We think so, too," Stevie said emphatically. After a pause, she added, "I'm sure Max would agree?" Her voice rose in a question at the end of the sentence.

"I'm sure of it," Deborah replied. "How could anyone not like Red?"

"Well—" Stevie began. Then she stopped herself. It was way too complicated a situation to go into with Max's fiancée. And if she said anything, she'd have to explain how she happened to know Max was going to be away the second week of camp. "Well, that's a good question," she concluded lamely. The relieved

77

looks on Carole's and Lisa's faces showed that they thought she had made the right choice not to say anything.

Deborah had left her car parked behind the stable so that there would be less chance of Max's noticing it. She walked back to it with The Saddle Club. "I had such a good lesson that I'm bubbling over," she confided. "I'll have to watch out at work. Supposedly I'm out here investigating a horse-switching scam."

"There's a horse-switching scam going on?" Lisa asked. Having worked for a local newspaper herself, she was fascinated with Deborah's reporter job.

"I guess you could say that. A couple of days ago I rode Barq, but today Red switched me to Delilah," Deborah joked.

Stevie looked at Deborah with newfound respect. Somehow Deborah's sneaking out to Pine Hollow to take riding lessons sounded a lot like skipping class to do extracurricular activities. She hadn't realized that adults were capable of such intelligent planning.

THE FOLLOWING SUNDAY afternoon, the threesome decided to take a trail ride. The mood around Pine Hollow was tense. They could sense that there were a lot of secrets in the air, and not all of them were good. There were rumors flying—about Max and Deborah, about camp, about Veronica and Red. Judging from the whispered conversations in the tack room and indoor ring, The Saddle Club weren't the only ones wondering why Red wasn't going to be instructing at camp.

After schooling on the flat, the girls set off at an easy walk, glad to escape the dusty ring. Schooling was important, but taking a breather was, too. Horses that spent too much time in the ring could get bored, just like kids who got sick of school. Besides, riders could learn as much from hacking outside as from drilling in the ring. Trail riding was a great time to get used to riding over different terrain, splashing through water puddles, and hopping over small obstacles such as fallen trees.

The great thing about a trail ride was that it was a way for a horse and rider to relax and have fun. Some of The Saddle Club's most memorable adventures had taken place on the trail.

Starlight, Prancer, and Belle knew the route to Willow Creek by heart, so Carole, Lisa, and Stevie loosened the reins, relaxed, and talked. By mutual consent they had decided not to mention any of the not-so-wonderful things going on. They were doing their best to help Red, and, until the representative from the Equestrian Center came, they would just have to be patient.

When they got to the creek, the three of them tied their horses and sat at the water's edge. They all took off their riding boots and rolled up their pants so they could dangle their feet in the cool stream. In the hot Virginia summer the creek was always a favorite spot.

"This water just reminded me: What's left to plan for the Bath?" Carole asked.

Lisa reached into her pocket and withdrew a folded piece of yellow legal paper. "I think we're almost all set," she said. "For food and drinks we've got people signed up to bring brownies, oatmeal-raisin cookies, tortilla chips with salsa, cheese popcorn, root beer, ginger ale—oh, and, ah, Jell-O."

"Jell-O?" Carole and Stevie repeated in unison.

Lisa gave a sheepish smile. "Simon Atherton told me it was his absolute favorite food, and I didn't have the heart to tell him not to bring it."

Carole and Stevie nodded understandingly. Simon was one of the stranger students who rode at Pine Hollow. There was nothing exactly *wrong* with him, he just seemed to march to his own drummer. Evidence of this was that he had a persistent crush on Veronica despite the fact that she had repeatedly been as rude as humanly possible to him.

"How about decorations?" Stevie inquired. "I hope whoever volunteered is prepared to turn the tack room into a thing of beauty."

The girls had decided that cleaning out the tack room was the best solution for the setting of the Groom's Bath. "We have two riders who have sworn to buy out all the streamers at the mall," Lisa answered, checking her list. "If all goes as planned, we'll just have to set up and supervise on the actual day.

Oh, wait, I forgot one thing: We still have to think up a theme for the presents. A lot of kids have been asking me what to get Max."

"I noticed his tack was getting kind of worn out. Why don't we all pitch in and buy him a new bridle at the tack shop?" Carole suggested.

Stevie and Lisa looked at each other, eyebrows raised. Finally Stevie said, "Are you going to say it, or am I?"

Before they could decide, Carole jumped in. "Just because we give Max a bridle doesn't make this a bridal shower!" she exclaimed, exasperated.

"Anyway, the point is, we have to give him gifts that will be appropriate for a man who is about to get married, not for a man who is about to go hacking," Lisa pointed out. "I did look up 'showers' in my mother's book on manners to see what was acceptable, but somehow tea towels and place mats don't seem right."

"I can't even imagine what a tea towel is, let alone Max using it," Stevie said.

"Yeah, it's funny, but I guess Max does do things like eat breakfast, doesn't he?" Carole asked.

Because they always saw Max in the stables—riding, teaching, or training—sometimes it was hard for the girls to imagine him doing normal, everyday things.

"I wonder who will do the cooking," Lisa mused idly, splashing water over her ankles and calves. "Deborah's career takes up at least as much time as Max's, and she'll have to commute to the city."

"That's it!" Stevie cried suddenly. Carole and Lisa were all ears. "Deborah is giving Max the gift of learning to ride so that she can share in his career. Maybe Max should learn something about the newspaper business in return."

"So the theme for the Bath would be—journalism?" Carole asked.

"Right. Everyone will have to bring something to do with Deborah's job as a reporter," Stevie said. She paused, letting the other two absorb the idea.

"I like it," Carole said. "Besides, it's the least Deborah deserves, after working so hard to surprise Max."

"I know—we could bring things like copies of books by investigative reporters," Lisa said.

"Yeah, and then the tools of an investigative reporter . . . say, a magnifying glass," Stevie said.

"Lock picks—for breaking into rooms!" Carole added.

"Fake IDs!"

"Reporters' notepads!"

"A mini–tape recorder!"

"A tube to put up against the wall so you can hear through it, fingerprint dusting powder, a camera that looks like a fountain pen!"

Lisa looked doubtfully at Stevie. "Stevie, have you been watching too many old detective movies?"

"We-ell, I did catch a triple feature last weekend," Stevie confessed.

Lisa hastily scribbled some of their ideas on the back of her party list so that they could make suggestions to the other riders. None of them was sure how many of the things they had thought of actually existed, but they *were* positive that everyone would have fun choosing them.

"And what's most important, Max may not actually need any of the silly gifts he'll be getting, but at least he'll enjoy opening them," Carole concluded.

"The theme should make Deborah laugh, too. And that's what a party's for, right?" Lisa said.

With the Bath planned, The Saddle Club was ready to make the leisurely trip back to Pine Hollow. They felt cool and refreshed, mentally and physically.

The feeling did not last long. When they reached the stable yard, they saw the diAngelos' white Mercedes parked outside Max's office.

"Why is it that whenever I see that car, I just know they're up to something bad?" Lisa remarked.

"I don't know, but you don't have to be an investigative reporter to come to that conclusion," Stevie said dryly.

The three of them dismounted and were heading into the barn when Mrs. diAngelo appeared, followed by a sulking Veronica. "It's not fair, Mother! You and Max think you can get away with ignoring me! But I'm going to win in the end!"

"Keep your voice down," Mrs. diAngelo snapped. "You're making a scene!"

In response, Veronica swung her foot back and kicked the front tire of the Mercedes as hard as she could. Mrs. diAngelo fixed her with an iron expression. "Your father will speak to Max as soon as he comes home from his business trip. We will discuss *your* behavior later," she said icily. "Now get into the car." Pouting, Veronica flounced over to the passenger side and got in. As she did, she caught a glimpse of Lisa, Carole, and Stevie, all of whom were staring at her. She sneered at them, then slammed the car door hard.

The three girls watched the sleek white car disappear down the driveway. Carole was the first to speak. "Do you think it's good or bad that Veronica and her mother are in a fight over something that's going on at Pine Hollow?"

"And what is Mr. diAngelo going to speak to Max about?" Lisa asked.

"And why is Max ignoring Veronica?" Stevie said.

Without saying it, they were all sure that Veronica's attacks on Red must have somehow been the cause of the scene they had just witnessed. But before they could answer any of their own questions, Red emerged from the stable. He nodded briefly to them and then hurried toward his truck. A minute later he, too, disappeared down the driveway.

"First the diAngelos storm off, then Red rushes out? What on earth could be going on?" Lisa demanded.

Carole sighed, leaning against Starlight. "I don't know, but this day is getting more confusing than a tangled four-in-hand harness."

9

STEVIE WAS THE first to arrive for class on Tuesday. On the way over, she had tried to think of something she could say to Max that would make him want to reveal his wedding and honeymoon plans. Once he had made an announcement about the cruise, she would feel okay about asking why he wasn't leaving Red in charge as usual. But she didn't want to bring up the subject herself, because she would have to admit to snooping on Max's desk, and it also might sound as if she didn't like Denise. Everyone agreed that Denise was wonderful; the point was how unfair it was for Max to pick *anyone* over Red.

She had tried the joking approach already. Hinting

about the wedding and the cruise hadn't worked. Now Stevie thought she might be able to engage Max in a casual conversation, which she could then turn toward the wedding. She went directly to his office and rapped lightly on the door.

"Yes?" Max said, looking up from his paperwork.

"Hi, Max," Stevie said, trying to make her voice sound normal. She sat down on the sofa and picked up a horse magazine. "Great weather for our lesson, isn't it?"

"Is there something you need, Stevie?" Max asked, his voice testy. He glanced at his watch distractedly, stood up, and began to stack the mess on his desk into neat piles.

"Oh, are you in a hurry?" Stevie asked. "There's plenty of time until the lesson."

"I realize that, Stevie, but I have a few things to take care of, all right? If you need to talk to me, say so."

Stevie stared openmouthed at her riding instructor. Max was acting more irritable than she'd seen him in a long, long time. She was about to make another attempt at conversation. Then she thought better of it. With the diAngelos and Red to worry about, and his own plans to consider, Max obviously had a lot on his mind. Before he could get more worked up, Stevie murmured something about being glad that Denise was going to teach at camp, and slipped out the door.

To her surprise, Max called after her. "Stevie! I'm sorry. I didn't mean to snap at you. See you in the lesson, okay?"

Now Stevie was really astonished. It was one thing for Max to get annoyed with her for pestering him. It was quite another for him to *apologize* for getting annoyed. In fact, Stevie could count on one hand— maybe even on a couple of fingers—the number of times Max had said he was sorry to her. Backing away, she gave him the best smile she could manage and then hurried to the stalls to find Lisa and Carole.

"You look like you've seen a ghost," Lisa commented when she saw Stevie's face. She had Prancer cross-tied in the aisle and was currying the mare vigorously. Carole had stationed Starlight one pair of cross-ties down so that she could talk with Lisa while they groomed.

"Actually, I saw something weirder," Stevie said. "I went to try to get Max into a conversation about his wedding, but before I could get two words in, he nearly bit my head off."

"That's weird?" Carole asked. She pulled a few long hairs out of Starlight's perfectly kept mane.

"No, that's normal—or close to it. The thing that spooked me is that he apologized for snapping at me."

Both Carole and Lisa stopped grooming and looked at Stevie. "Boy, this Red-Veronica thing must really be bothering him," Carole said, her voice sympathetic.

"The poor guy is trying to make plans for marrying the woman he loves, and instead he has to worry about Veronica's stupid accusations," Lisa said.

"Yeah, it's no wonder he's not himself," Stevie agreed. "Any sign of the Equestrian Center examiner?" she asked hopefully. She and Carole and Lisa had gotten into the habit of scanning the driveway for strange cars.

"Nope. The only cars in the driveway are Max's, Red's, and Mrs. Reg's. And I guess that means you haven't heard anything by mail?" Lisa asked.

Stevie shook her head. "I check the mailbox every day, though," she said glumly. Stevie left to get Belle ready. She didn't want to risk another run-in with Max, this time about being late. She stopped by the tack room on her way to the mare's stall. Startled, she saw Max standing inside. He was staring blankly at the row of saddles.

Stevie entered the room quietly and grabbed her tack. Max looked at her and smiled vaguely. Stevie didn't feel like waiting around for him to snap out of whatever daze he was in. He had said he had lots of things to take care of before the lesson. Evidently, one of them was gazing at saddles.

WHEN THE LESSON started, Max called the group into the center of the ring. Veronica straggled up, the last to arrive. She grabbed her reins from Red, who had been holding Garnet at ringside, waiting to give Veronica a leg up. Without a word of greeting, the girl put her foot into Red's hands and sprang into the saddle. Max looked at her disapprovingly but said nothing. "Uh, today we'll be working on relaxation of the horse and rider," he announced.

The Saddle Club exchanged glances.

"We're working on it again, you mean?" Lisa asked timidly. Normally she wouldn't have questioned Max, but today he looked plain out of it.

Max frowned. "How silly of me. Of course, we did that last week. What I meant to say is, ah . . . is . . . why doesn't everyone warm up using the exercises we learned last week. I know you've been practicing them on your own, and I want to see your progress."

That sounded better. The riders filed out to the rail and began to go through the stretches they had

91

learned. Max watched for a few minutes without saying anything. Then Mrs. Reg appeared at the rail of the ring and summoned him over. "Your suit has come back from the cleaners," Lisa overheard the older woman tell Max.

The rest of the warm-up went haphazardly. Max seemed to be looking at his watch more than at his students. Carole noticed that a couple of times Veronica snatched at Garnet's reins without provoking so much as a mild reprimand from Max. He stared right at her, then glanced away. It made Carole worry to see Max this way. She had seen him distracted, but now he seemed almost nervous.

"Mrs. diAngelo must have really gotten to him," she whispered to Lisa, who had trotted up beside her.

"I know! I was waiting for him to yell at Veronica, and he ignored her completely," Lisa responded. "If this goes on every day until his wedding, I don't think I'll be able to take it."

By reflex, they glanced anxiously at Max to see if he had noticed them talking, but he seemed lost in thought.

NEAR THE END of the lesson, Deborah came out to the ring. She waved to The Saddle Club, who waved back. Max seemed delighted to see her. He interrupted the lesson, gave her a big kiss, and spoke with her for several minutes.

"She sure gets his mind off his worries, doesn't she? That's the most relaxed he's seemed during the entire lesson," Lisa said.

"You call this a lesson?" Stevie asked. "I call it the 'everyone come talk to Max' hour."

"You can't blame him for wanting to talk to his fiancée. Half the time she comes, she sneaks in and out without even saying hi," Lisa said.

It was nice to see Max as half of a happy couple. The two of them talked and joked until Deborah left. Then Max seemed to remember himself. He shouted out a few commands to wake everyone up. But right as they got going, Mrs. Reg reappeared at the ring. Max seemed to realize that it was hopeless to try to continue the class for the remaining five minutes. He told everyone to pack it in for the day, and joined his mother at the rail. The two of them began to speak in hushed tones.

Meanwhile, Veronica, who had dismounted, began to holler for Red. Red showed up in a couple of minutes, walking hurriedly.

"I haven't got all day," Veronica said loudly. "And Garnet's ears and muzzle need to be trimmed. They're getting all gross and hairy."

Red started to explain. "We trim the whiskers on all the horses at the same—"

"I don't care when *all* the horses get done," Veronica cut him off. "I care only about Garnet, and I'm telling you to trim her whiskers today. Got it?"

Watching her rebuke Red for something that was beyond his control was too much for Carole. She felt anger at Veronica boiling over inside her. It wasn't fair that one person should have so much control over another person. Without thinking about what she was doing, she opened her mouth and yelled at Veronica. "Just quit it! Stop telling Red what to do!"

Veronica gaped at Carole. Her face flushed an angry red. "How dare you interfere in something that's not your business?" she demanded, her voice trembling.

Red motioned for Carole to keep out of it, but she was too wound up. It seemed as if she had been watching Veronica attack Red forever. Suddenly she couldn't tolerate it. She stood her ground. "This happens to *be* my business—and everyone else's at Pine Hollow. You've been unfairly criticizing Red for too long, and we're sick of it."

Lisa and Stevie, impressed with Carole's courage, immediately backed her up. Stevie stood beside Carole while Lisa went to the rail to get Max's attention. The three of them were so bent on telling Veronica off that none of them noticed the irritated expression on Red's face.

"Max," Lisa began, tugging on his sleeve, "we all think Red is great with the horses—I can't believe you wouldn't—I mean, he's one of the best employees anyone could have," she blurted out. She knew she wasn't making sense, but she was too worked up to slow down and speak calmly.

Mrs. Reg and Max looked at her curiously. "I'm fully aware of all of Red's capabilities," Max said sternly, turning back to his mother.

Lisa didn't know what to say to that. Max had taken all the wind out of her argument. She glanced anxiously back at Carole and Stevie. Carole seemed to have won round one, for Veronica had stormed off toward her mother's waiting car.

"What happened?" Lisa asked breathlessly, joining the others. Carole and Stevie looked at her, embarrassed.

Red spoke up. "Listen, I know you're trying to help, but I don't need you to stand up for me or to tell Max that I'm doing my job, okay?" he said gruffly.

"But, Red, that's what *you* think. Just when someone becomes the most confident, that's when they won't notice what's *really* going on," Stevie said urgently. She didn't want to annoy Red more, but the situation was getting desperate. The Equestrian Center seemed to be ignoring their letter, and Veronica, backed by her parents, was getting worse every day, while Max was turning into a wimp.

"Yes, well, I'll deal with anything that comes up," Red replied. Leading Garnet, he headed toward the barn.

Carole waited until he was gone a few minutes. Then she cried, "How could I have been so dumb? We made Red look stupid in front of Veronica."

"Hey, I'm the one who went to Max," Lisa said. She let her breath out in a long sigh. "A lot of good that did."

"All right—no getting upset about this. We're just trying to help Red. If he can't appreciate that . . ." Stevie's voice trailed off.

Carole looked at her quizzically. "If he can't appreciate that, then what?"

"Well, too bad. Because our help is far from over," Stevie said. "And when he passes the Equestrian Center test, he'll change his tune fast."

"I hope so," Carole said. "I think Veronica and I were on the brink of a fistfight!"

As they walked the horses back, Deborah emerged from the stable. "I was hoping you'd be coming in about now," she said. "I've got a favor to ask. Could you think of something to distract Max while I have another riding lesson?"

"That's easy," Stevie said. "He's been totally distracted all afternoon."

Deborah laughed. "It doesn't surprise me."

After a quick Saddle Club conference, they decided that Carole and Lisa would put Belle away while Stevie found a way to occupy Max. Deborah thanked them and hurried off to change from her city reporter's clothes into riding attire.

Stevie racked her brains for the perfect foil. She gazed out at the driveway. A grain delivery truck had just pulled out and was waiting to let a flower delivery truck pull in. Stevie remembered hearing Mrs. Reg say something about needing to spruce up the jump course with some shrubbery. That didn't help her think of anything. Then the grain delivery truck sparked her memory. She remembered a point Denise had made in her nutrition lecture. She clapped her hands together. She had it—the perfect distraction. She made a few preparations and went to find Max. Once again he was sitting in his office.

"I'm sorry to bother you, Max, but there's something I think you should look at. You know how Denise was telling us that it's very important to look at the quality of each new grain shipment that comes in?" Stevie asked.

"Of course. That was a very important point she made," Max said.

"Well, for practice I went and looked at the shipment we just got, and I don't think the sweet feed is the same quality as the stuff we usually feed."

Max raised his eyebrows. "Really? That's serious. I'll go check it out." Instead of seeming annoyed by the interruption, Max almost looked eager to have something to do. Stevie watched happily as he set off for the grain room. There she had set out eight buckets of grain for him to examine. To keep him busy, she had mixed in the remains of her lunch—a few crumbled-up cookies, a lettuce leaf or two, and a couple of sandwich crusts. When she peeked around the grain room door, she saw Max crouching beside the buckets, wearing a puzzled expression. She had to clamp her hand over her mouth to keep from cracking up. Max normally would have dispensed with her trickery in about two minutes. But today Max was being so flaky that she knew the hoax would keep him busy for at least the length of the riding lesson. Grinning impishly, she went to help Lisa and Carole.

When she got to Belle's stall, the mare was inside, cool and groomed. There was a note stuck to her nameplate: *Gone to watch. Come join us when finished. L and C.* She tore the note off, gave Belle a good pat, and headed out to the schooling ring.

Lisa and Carole were perched on the rail. "She's doing really well," Carole whispered to Stevie as she climbed up. Stevie quickly filled them in on the grain hoax and then settled in to watch.

In the ring, Deborah was cantering Delilah. It was clear that she had learned a lot. She looked fairly confident in the saddle. The wind had picked up, and her red ponytail bounced on her back. When Red told her to trot, she sat up and steadied the mare with her seat, legs, and hands. Delilah broke evenly into a trot. Deborah sat quietly for a few seconds and then began to post. She started off on the wrong diagonal but quickly corrected herself. Red praised her for noticing the mistake.

"She looks a hundred times better," Stevie murmured.

"Thanks to Red's being such a great teacher," said Lisa. They all knew that Deborah's own motivation was a big part of her success, but that was a given. Red had taken her from a total beginner to someone who had the basics down pat. She could walk, trot, and canter, change leads, and post correctly. That was more than enough to be able to join Max on a trail ride or school with him in the ring.

The sound of a car pulling into the driveway interrupted The Saddle Club's thoughts. They had gotten so used to noting every single car that drove onto the property that they turned automatically. "Hey, I've never seen that car before," Lisa said. It was a dark blue sedan.

As they watched, the car stopped and a well-dressed woman got out, carrying some papers and a notebook. She looked around vaguely. Stevie squinted in the sun, trying to see if she recognized the woman. Then she did a double take. The car had an Indiana license plate!

BECAUSE HER SIGNATURE was first on the letter, Stevie figured she should be the first to introduce herself. As she trotted over she could barely catch her breath, she was so excited. It was perfect! Red was already in the middle of giving a lesson, so the test could start right away.

"You're the judge, aren't you?" she asked excitedly.

"Yes—yes, I am," the woman said. She seemed a bit taken aback by Stevie's enthusiasm.

"We're so happy you could make it!" Stevie exclaimed.

"Naturally I could make it. It's my job, after all," the woman replied.

"It's just that Pine Hollow is so far away. We were worried you might not come," Stevie explained.

"It's not *that* far," the woman said. "Believe me, I've gone much farther." She looked Stevie up and down. "And, ah, who might you be?" she asked.

"I'm Stephanie Lake," Stevie said.

"And what exactly is your role in all this?" the woman asked.

"I take riding lessons at Pine Hollow, board my horse here, do Pony Club—everything, I guess you could say, so I've really gotten a great chance to get to know the people who work here," Stevie said.

"How nice for you," the woman said vaguely.

Stevie felt that some explanation was in order. "If I seem a little overenthusiastic, it's because we've been waiting and waiting for you."

The judge gave her a look. "Really? But I'm right on time," she said.

"You've got that right," Stevie said. "We couldn't have asked for better timing." Another couple of days, she thought to herself, and Red might have been gone.

The judge looked through her stack of papers quickly. "Well, I guess I'm all ready to go. Where is the lucky man?"

Stevie pointed to the schooling ring, where Carole

102

and Lisa were waiting in anticipation. "He's right out there, teaching a lesson."

"Oh, I see. Teaching riding must be *very* important to him," the judge observed, half smiling.

"It is. He's a wonderful instructor," Stevie gushed.

"And is that the fiancée?" the judge asked.

"The fiancée?" Stevie repeated.

"Yes, riding the horse," the judge said.

"That's right," Stevie said. She was amazed that the woman had done so much preliminary research that she knew about Red's present to Deborah. Then again, the more the examiner knew about Red, the less they would have to fill her in on his character.

There was an awkward pause. The woman seemed to be waiting for Stevie to say something. "All right, then," the judge said finally, "why don't we get them to come over here."

Stevie was ready for this. After they had hurt Red's pride by trying to stand up for him, she wasn't about to let him know what was going on until the test was finished and his certification was a done deed. That way he couldn't get annoyed. "Oh, no," she said. "It's really better if you stay over here. They'd both appreciate it—better for the nerves, you know," she said.

The judge looked skeptical but said, "I do know

how nervous some people get. But the procedure doesn't take long at all."

Stevie thought for a minute. Unable to contain their curiosity any longer, Carole and Lisa came up and joined her. They introduced themselves politely. "When's it going to start?" Carole asked.

"Why, as soon as possible," the judge said.

"I was just explaining to the judge that Red would be happier if she stayed over here," Stevie said, elbowing the two of them.

Catching on right away, Lisa came to the rescue. "Oh, definitely. When it's all over, Red will thank you."

"Besides," Carole put in, "if you stay here, you can see how perfectly the two of them work together. That's important, isn't it?"

"Certainly. But, really, there are some formalities to be observed. I have a few questions to ask them," the woman said firmly.

"Oh, that's no problem. We can answer any questions you have," Stevie said.

"You can?" the woman asked.

The girls nodded. "You see, we've known Red for years and years," Lisa said.

"Well, all right," the judge said dubiously. She took

out her book and began to fill in spaces. "What did you say the man's name was?"

"Red O'Malley," Stevie answered promptly.

The judge looked surprised. "Is that some kind of a nickname? It doesn't sound like what I was told."

"Oh, of course!" Carole exclaimed. "How could we be so silly. It's *Redford* O'Malley. That's his full name."

Lisa and Stevie exchanged glances, relieved. They had completely forgotten about changing Red's name in the letter. Carole's quick thinking had saved them.

But the woman frowned. "That doesn't sound right either," she said.

"Yes, it's a strange name—a family name," Lisa said as casually as she could. She sneaked a look at Carole and Stevie. They looked as ill as she felt. Not only were they certifying Red without his knowing it, they were also making up names for him.

After an agonizing pause, the judge shrugged and wrote down "Redford O'Malley." Then she asked, "And the fiancée?"

"You have to know her name too?" Stevie said. "She's just a beginning student."

"Whether she's a beginner or an Olympian makes no difference to me," the woman said, starting to sound exasperated. "I still need to know her name."

105

"It's Deborah Hale," Lisa supplied hastily. She shot a warning glance at Stevie. The less fuss they made, the more quickly Red would be certified. Now was no time to question the judge's demands.

"So, I guess you'd better get started, huh?" Carole suggested. They were all petrified that Max would appear at any minute and ask what was going on. Then Red would be embarrassed again, since it was none of his doing, and their whole plan to help him would be ruined.

"I suppose so. Although it's going to be very difficult to communicate. The whole thing is highly irregular." The woman paused to sigh. "People get stranger and stranger—they want to do it all sorts of ways these days."

"Listen," Lisa began, thinking on her feet. "We could relay the information back and forth. It will be much more accurate that way."

"Accurate?" the judge asked. "I would think just the opposite."

"No, you see, if you stood by the rail, they would both get nervous, and you wouldn't see them as they really are. This way, they'll stay as relaxed as always," Lisa said.

"I suppose that makes sense," the judge agreed finally. "I'm not eager to get my suit dirty, and it seems to be quite dusty in the ring with all the wind. I must say, I wasn't expecting them to be having a riding lesson when I arrived."

"So, you usually start off unmounted?" Carole asked with curiosity. She wanted to understand the certification process as fully as she could in case she was ever up for it.

"Of course we usually start off unmounted!" the judge snapped. "And finish that way, too!"

Carole bit her lip. She hadn't realized it was such a stupid question, but now that she thought about it, she realized that the examiner would naturally want to see how the candidate started his lesson—whether he could teach his students to tack up and mount, two of the most fundamental elements of riding.

"But in this case," the judge continued haughtily, "I suppose I'll have to make an exception."

Lisa jumped in. "Great, then we can begin whenever you're ready," she said. She knew these examiners could be extremely picky about running things their way, and she didn't want to give the judge a chance to change her mind. She and Carole and Stevie spread out in a fireman's chain between the judge and the ring with Lisa closest to the judge.

It seemed like a good idea, but the minute the woman asked her first question, Lisa knew that there was a problem with her plan. With the high winds, she could barely hear the judge. The human "telephone" was a bad connection. Lisa made a split-second decision not to say anything. Max could figure out Stevie's prank any minute and come to find out what they were all doing. It just wasn't worth the risk.

The first thing the judge asked was some lengthy question having to do with Deborah's wanting to spend time with Red. Obviously the center was interested in finding out if the instructor was popular with his students. "Just ask Deborah if she thinks Red is a good teacher!" Lisa yelled. Carole and Stevie passed the question down the line to Deborah.

Deborah looked surprised by the sudden interruption of her lesson, but she responded with a resounding yes. Red glowered at Stevie, the closest to the ring, but continued with the lesson. So far, so good, Stevie thought. Obviously Red thought that the question was a stupid reason to disrupt the lesson, but there was no way he could have guessed what it was leading to.

When the next question came, it sounded to Lisa like "Mumble, jumble, blah, blah, Redford O'Malley, blah, blah, blah." Trying to keep Red's annoyance to a minimum, she shouted, "Just tell Red to say yes!"

Stevie tried, but Red walked angrily over to the rail. "What are all these questions about?" he called.

"Routine testing!" Stevie called back, hoping it sounded okay. She knew that Red would want to avoid disrupting Deborah's lesson at all costs, and she was betting on that to keep him relatively quiet.

"Can't it wait?" Red cried.

"Sorry, no—the woman has to leave as soon as possible!" Stevie yelled.

Red shook his head in disgust but said nothing further.

Then, all at once, two things happened. Max came out of the stable and headed for Stevie, a menacing expression on his face, and a huge gust of wind whipped through Pine Hollow.

The strange scene Max saw stopped him in his tracks: His fiancée was taking a riding lesson with his head stable hand, The Saddle Club was standing in a line, yelling to one another, and a well-dressed adult whom he had never seen before was trying desperately to hold on to a stack of loose papers that were fluttering all over the place. Registering all these particulars, Max's expression changed from pleasant surprise to annoyed curiosity to total confusion.

As he stared, dumbfounded, the gust picked up one of the woman's papers. She swatted at it but missed. It floated high in the air above the girls' heads. Carole reached up and snatched it. She scanned a few paragraphs, hoping to find some information about the sneaky questions the judge would be asking Red when they got to the hard part. But when she realized what she was holding, she let out a shriek. It was a nearly complete State of Virginia marriage certificate, uniting Red O'Malley and Deborah Hale in matrimony!

The next question came from the judge. Lisa yelled to them to tell Red to say yes once again. Carole stood frozen, staring at the certificate. In the back of her mind she heard Stevie instructing Red to say yes.

"No!" Carole yelled at the top of her lungs.

"No what?" Stevie cried.

"Tell Red to say no!" Carole shouted.

"But I just told him to say yes!" As she yelled to Carole, Stevie suddenly caught sight of Max. He was running toward them. The examination would fail unless Red answered at once. "Red—say yes!" Stevie yelled.

At the same time, Carole hollered, "Red—say no!"

And that's what he said, just in the nick of time.

"No, no, no—I will not answer any more questions until somebody tells me what on earth is going on!" Red declared.

"Exactly what I was going to ask," Max said, rushing up.

The judge folded her arms across her chest expectantly.

The Saddle Club ran to join the group. Explanations started bubbling. Nobody seemed to know who had the answers. Hearing the commotion, Denise emerged from the stables, bridle pieces, saddle soap, and sponge in hand. When she saw the group, she hurried over. "Is anything wrong?" she asked.

"We're waiting to find out," Max replied.

Red managed to get the floor first. "As far as I'm concerned, I was just trying to give Deborah her wedding present," he said.

Deborah looked down at Max, embarrassed, from Delilah's back. "Thanks to Red's generosity, I was just trying to learn to ride before our wedding. Red is teaching me, and I've had to take lessons whenever the two of us could squeeze them in. It was supposed to be a secret from you until we were married."

Max gazed up at Deborah, delighted with the news. For a moment the two smiled at each other as everyone else suddenly found something fascinating to look at off in the distance. Then Max remembered the rest of the day's activities. "So that explains why—"

"Why I had to distract you for an hour while Deborah rode," Stevie finished for him, "by making up a ridiculous story about the grain being bad—"

"—and emptying the contents of your lunch into the grain buckets to keep me occupied," Max said, trying to get the last word.

"Hey, it worked, didn't it?" Stevie said, grinning.

"Anyway, during the lesson the 'judge' arrived," Carole continued.

"That much makes sense," Max said.

"Only our 'judge' was supposed to be here to certify Red as a Riding Counselor, just like Denise."

"A what?" Red asked, astonished.

"I was?" the judge exclaimed simultaneously.

Lisa cleared her throat and looked at Red. "We were trying to get you certified as a Riding Counselor so that Veronica would get off your back and then Max wouldn't believe all the awful things she said." She looked up at Red, steeling herself for the worst.

But instead of being annoyed, Red looked shyly pleased. "I guess I never appreciated the lengths you three were willing to go to in order to help me out," he said quietly.

Then they all started talking at once, filling in details for each other. Soon it all became very clear to everyone—except the poor judge. She had been standing quietly, listening to everyone's explanation. Finally she threw up her hands in confusion. "Excuse me," she said. Her low, authoritative judge's voice put a halt to the chatter. "I am Judge Emily Stilwell," she said. "Just exactly what does this riding certificate have to do with marriage, and exactly who *is* getting married today?"

"Today? Nobody's getting married *today*," said Stevie. "Max and Deborah are getting married on the twenty-seventh!"

"We are?" Deborah asked, surprised.

Stevie suddenly got a sinking feeling in her stomach. "You're not?"

"No, we're getting married today," Max said, looking slightly alarmed.

"Then who is marrying Redford O'Malley?" the judge demanded.

"Redford?" Red said.

"If you mean Red," Denise spoke up, "then that would be me, I think, but probably not for a couple of years and certainly not until Red gets up the guts to ask me." She slipped her arm through the stable hand's while Red blushed the color of his name.

This was too much for Stevie. She had thought that *she* knew all the secrets while everyone else was in the dark. Now it turned out that she had the date wrong for Max and Deborah's wedding *and* she had completely missed a blossoming Pine Hollow romance. It really wasn't fair.

"But you don't even know each other!" Stevie blurted out.

"Yes, we do," Denise said calmly. "Red and I met this spring at the university. Red's been taking equine studies classes there. Didn't you know?"

"And you really might marry each other?" Lisa asked, awestruck.

114

"Well . . . ," Deborah started to say, taking a side-long glance at Red.

"But he's about three-quarters married already," Judge Stilwell protested.

"To *my* fiancée," Max retorted.

"Will someone please tell me what's going on?" the judge asked.

"Have you ever heard of The Saddle Club, Your Honor?" Max began.

". . . SO NATURALLY, WHEN we saw the Indiana plates
on your car—" Stevie said, finally reaching the end of
a long explanation. The group had moved from the
schooling ring to the yard in front of the Regnerys'
house, where they could sit down.

"My sister-in-law is visiting me, and my car's in the
shop," Judge Stilwell explained.

"She is?" Stevie asked. "I mean, it is?"

"I'm afraid so," the judge said sympathetically. "But
I'm flattered that you thought I knew enough about
horses to examine a riding instructor. I've never actually set foot on a horse farm before."

At that moment, Mrs. Reg swung open the door of

116

the house. She was wearing a huge apron over a matching peach-colored blouse and skirt. Her hair was swept into an attractive bun. "It looks like you're having an important conversation," she called, "but the frosting on the cake is beginning to slip, and if we're going to have a wedding, we'd best have it now!"

Max, Deborah, and the judge stood up to go into the house. Stevie cleared her throat. Max stopped. He tried to look severe but ended up grinning from ear to ear. "You know, I thought I was going to have a chance to do something in my life without having The Saddle Club in my hair," he said. "But it looks like that won't happen. If I don't let you girls witness the wedding, you'll probably find a way to try to marry my wife off to someone else! So you'd better come on in. Red, you and Denise should join us, too. Mom? Is there enough cake for a few more guests?"

"Plenty," said Mrs. Reg. "Somehow I always knew that threesome would find a way to be at the wedding!"

With that, everyone streamed into the house. Deborah dashed upstairs while Max fled to a back room. In the kitchen, Carole, Lisa, and Stevie hugged one another with joy. Despite all the mishaps and all their mistaken assumptions, they were going to see Max get married after all.

"I guess we'll have to wear our riding clothes," Lisa said. "They're all we've got."

Mrs. Reg surveyed the three of them critically. "Go into my room upstairs, wash up, and wait for me."

The girls did as they were told, happily splashing water on their faces and redoing their hair. In a few minutes, Mrs. Reg appeared, carrying a pile of clothes. "If you're going to wear riding clothes, you might as well wear coats and stock ties," she said. "See if any of these fit. Some are Max's old stuff; some were left here after shows."

The girls eagerly scrambled to try on the coats. Soon Stevie had found a dark gray, Lisa a black, and Carole a slightly too small hunter green. They lined up for Mrs. Reg to tie their ties.

"All right, everybody find a place in the living room now. They should be starting any minute," the older woman urged. She hurried down the stairs to the kitchen to oversee the final preparations.

Stevie and Carole followed her, but Lisa had another idea. "Back in a minute," she yelled, banging through the door. She ran to the locker room of the stable area, where she had her camera and a couple of rolls of film, then ran back.

"Thank goodness someone remembered to take pictures," said Mrs. Reg. "Thank you so much, Lisa."

118

Lisa went into the living room and stationed herself to get a good picture of the bride descending the stairs. Thanks to Mrs. Reg, the room looked perfect for a wedding. A number of vases held bouquets of pink roses mixed with baby's breath. Sunlight streamed in through the open windows. Quickly, Lisa snapped a shot of Stevie, Carole, Red, Denise, and Mrs. Reg. She snapped another of Max, standing alone, waiting for his bride. Then all eyes turned to the staircase. Deborah came down slowly, beautifully dressed in a simple beige silk suit. Max took her hands, and the small private ceremony began.

A few minutes later, Judge Emily Stilwell pronounced Maximillian Regnery III and Deborah Halby Hale husband and wife. After the applause died down, the judge turned to the group. "Now, you're sure I've married the right bride to the right groom?" she joked.

"Absolutely, positively, one hundred percent sure!" Max exclaimed, planting a kiss on Deborah's lips.

"Then on to the cake!" Mrs. Reg announced. She brought out the dessert, a two-tiered white cake with white icing and pink flowers. Red helped to carry out a bottle of chilled champagne and some ginger ale for the girls. First Mrs. Reg made a toast to Max's and Deborah's health. Immediately after that, everyone had a toast. Max toasted his wife's riding career; Deborah toasted Mrs. Reg's cake; Red toasted Denise, and she toasted him back; and The Saddle Club toasted themselves, since no one else had.

"I just wish my parents could have been here," Deborah murmured wistfully. "I know they couldn't leave London, but still . . ."

Max gave her hand a squeeze. "I know, but we'll see them soon," he answered.

When everyone was sitting down, happily munching cake, Stevie spoke up. "We're still curious about a couple of things."

"Better clear them up now," Max said with the air of someone about to tackle a huge project.

"Why did you get married today, when you don't leave for your honeymoon until the twenty-seventh?" Stevie asked.

"That's not true—we leave for our honeymoon tonight," Max said.

"But the cruise isn't until the twenty-eighth," Carole countered.

"The cruise? Oh, the cruise!" Max exclaimed. "Are you by any chance referring to the *Ocean Pearl*?"

The three girls nodded.

"*We're* not taking that cruise—my mother is," Max said. "She hasn't had a proper vacation in years, so

120

Deborah and I decided to give *her* a present. We're sending her on a Caribbean cruise."

Mrs. Reg nodded. "That's the truth, girls."

"Although how you would know about the cruise is beyond me," Max continued, grinning wickedly.

Stevie smiled wanly. "Let's just say I happened to find out about it."

"Right. And you happened to be snooping around my desk. And you happened to read, in detail, the cruise brochures on my desk."

"That's the way it happened," Stevie said. She elbowed Lisa, who was sitting beside her, and muttered, "Help me out here."

"So, Max," Lisa said promptly, "ah . . . let's see . . . oh, yeah, where are you and Deborah going on your honeymoon if you're not going on the cruise?"

"We're flying to London," Deborah answered. "My father is the chief of *The Washington Times* bureau in London, and so we'll get to see my parents as well as take a vacation. Of course, Max has to be back in time for camp, so we'll be gone only a week."

"Back for camp? Then that means you'll also be back in time for your Bath!" Carole cheered.

Deborah looked a little worried. "I expect Max will actually bathe before then."

121

Lisa glared at Carole. "You didn't have to give it away," she said.

"But since you have," Stevie continued, "we might as well tell Max that we've planned a wedding party for him."

"What does that have to do with bathing?" Max asked.

"Well, you see, we couldn't call it a bridal shower— or even a b-r-i-d-l-e shower, so then we thought, how about a *bath* instead of a *shower*, since it's for a groom instead of a bride," Lisa said.

To The Saddle Club's delight, everybody seemed to love the idea. Stevie was able to refrain—barely— from telling the theme.

Max promised not to miss the Bath. "In fact, it's all I'm going to think about my entire honeymoon," he said solemnly.

Deborah elbowed him hard.

"Max," said Mrs. Reg, "that's one vow you'd better not keep."

During the conversation, Red and Denise had slipped away into another room to look at the Regnerys' hunting prints. Their absence reminded Lisa that they had never asked Max an important question. A little timidly, she inquired, keeping her voice low, "Did you actually believe some of the stuff Veronica was saying about Red?"

To her relief, Max replied without hesitation. "Of course not. Red is the best stable hand I've ever had. And Denise is a great help, too. When I asked her to come teach at Pine Hollow, she wasn't sure she would. She was considering going back to Indiana for the summer. Then she started dating Red and decided to stay. So I'm thankful to him for that, too."

"But when did Red find the time to take equine studies classes?" Lisa asked.

"All spring, in the mornings, while you were in school, and now in the evenings after you go home. He also has to leave during the day occasionally for special meetings."

"We never knew that," Stevie said.

"Probably because you never asked, which"—Max paused to clear his throat—"you might have done before jumping to conclusions. That's why Red's not instructing at camp: He has his final examinations for the summer school session during the second week, and he has to prepare. But Denise and Red will be in charge while we're in London, and if Veronica doesn't like it, she can leave."

"But we thought the diAngelos were threatening you—telling you to fire Red," Carole said.

Max laughed out loud. "Boy, you must have really thought I was being a wimp! Actually, it's the opposite. I've had them in for a few meetings to discuss Veronica's behavior around here. If she doesn't shape up, she's not going to be allowed to come to camp."

In one motion, Stevie, Lisa, and Carole sat back on the sofa they were sharing. Their brains had reached information overload, and they couldn't absorb—or give—one more explanation. Max and Deborah rose and went to get their bags ready. Mrs. Reg began busying herself with the cleanup. Red and Denise reappeared in the doorway.

Lisa, whose logical mind couldn't rest until she knew every detail, made a superhuman effort to ask one remaining question. "By the way, Red," she said, "what *is* your real name?"

Red looked surprised. "I thought you knew," he said. "It's an old family name: Redford." He and Deborah clasped hands and headed out to the stable.

The three girls looked at one another and began to howl. They laughed until tears streamed down their faces. And then they laughed some more.

THE WEDDING WAS over, and the girls had helped Mrs. Reg do the few dishes. It was time for Max and Deborah to leave. Max brought their suitcases into the hall.

Deborah, who'd changed into her traveling clothes, joined him. They both embraced Mrs. Reg, whose face was the tiniest bit tearstained. "Max is her only son, and now he's married. I'm sure mothers think about days like this for years," Lisa whispered.

Then Stevie had an idea. She dashed out to the grain room. Everybody knew you weren't supposed to throw rice these days. It was bad for the birds that ate it because the rice expanded in their stomachs. So why not oats instead? She grabbed half a bucketful.

Lisa and Carole met her outside and scooped up handfuls of the grain. They waited, giggling, for the bride and groom. When Max and Deborah emerged from the house, the three girls showered them with handful after handful. Max grabbed Deborah's arm and they ran to her waiting car. "I knew I could count on you to do just one more ridiculous thing," Max said happily.

"But it's perfect, isn't it?" Stevie asked.

Max looked at the woman standing beside him. "Yes, it is," he said. They got in, and the car door closed. They were off.

CAROLE YAWNED AND turned over. This time, since the sleepover was at her house, she had the bed, and Lisa and Stevie were sharing the floor. She knew that she should enjoy her last chance to sleep in: Camp started tomorrow, and the riders had to be at Pine Hollow by eight every morning. Unfortunately, even though it was six A.M., she was wide awake.

"Carole, are you awake?" Lisa whispered.

"Yes."

"Oh, good. I've been dying to talk about the Bath, but I didn't want to wake you up."

"Why didn't you talk to *me*? I've been staring at the ceiling for half an hour," Stevie said indignantly. She

126

and Lisa climbed onto Carole's bed to get more comfortable.

The Bath had been a smashing success. Everyone who had volunteered had come through with great food and clever presents.

"You know, even Simon Atherton's Jell-O got eaten," Lisa said, giggling.

"Yeah, it was a real hit with the younger kids," said Carole.

"Didn't you love the look on Deborah's face when she suddenly figured out the theme of all of Max's presents?" Stevie asked.

Both Max and Deborah had been confused when they saw the first few gifts. "Dusting powder?" Max had asked. And then, "A mini–tape recorder?" Still, obviously not wanting to seem ungrateful, Max had thanked the gift givers. "I have to admit, though, I don't really understand what this stuff is used for."

"But, Max, it's obvious. The powder is for fingerprint dusting. The tape recorder is miniature so that you can record things without anyone knowing," Deborah explained.

"How do you know?" Max asked.

"Because all the gifts are"—she stopped for a split second, a slow smile spreading over her face—"they're

127

all things that have to do with investigative report-
ing," she finished, beaming.

"Oh, I see," Max said, "It's my turn to learn about
your career, huh?"

The Saddle Club had burst into applause. After
that, the newlyweds had practically pounced on the
remaining presents, tearing open a set of Sherlock
Holmes mysteries, a pair of walkie-talkies, a fake nose
and mustache disguise kit, and a guidebook to code
cracking. The final gift was from The Saddle Club. It
was a framed copy of the "Drug Ring at Local Track"
article that had brought Deborah in search of a horse
person to help her with the horsey details—namely,
Maximillian Regnery III. Deborah had choked up for
a minute. When she could speak again, she said, "And
to think it all started with a simple newspaper article."

After the gifts, the celebratory eating and talking
had continued most of the afternoon. Reluctantly
Max had said, "We all may be stuffed, but there are
some horses that need to be fed." And, in good Pine
Hollow style, they had all gone to help with the feeding.

"I'm not sure which was better," Carole said, sitting
up in bed, "the look on Deborah's face when she realized that the Bath presents were in her honor or the
look on Veronica's when she saw Red and Denise

holding hands last week. She stared at them so long, I thought her eyes would pop out of her head."

When Veronica had put two and two together and realized that her beloved Denise was dating Red, a very strange thing had happened. Whether because of that alone or because of that plus Max's threat about camp, Veronica's attitude toward Red had changed overnight. Now instead of yelling at him to take care of Garnet, she asked him to in a normal tone of voice. The Saddle Club had even overheard a "please" on at least two occasions. Of course they had made sure that Veronica knew all about Red's course of study at the university.

"So do you think this means that because someone with as many qualifications as Denise sees something to admire in Red, then perhaps he is good enough to groom Veronica's horse?" Lisa asked with mock seriousness.

"I don't know. Maybe if he gets a Ph.D. in equine studies, he'll be fit to touch one or two hairs on the horse," Stevie replied.

"I guess that's more likely than his ever becoming a Certified Riding Counselor with the Equestrian Center," Carole said.

"Oh, I almost forgot!" Stevie reached for her bag

and fumbled in it. She withdrew a letter, unfolded it, smoothed it out on her knees, and began to read: "Dear Stephanie Lake," the letter went. "Thank you very much for your interest in our Riding Counselor Certification program. I regret to inform you that the Equestrian Center is a state organization, not a national one. We can therefore certify only those instructors living and working in Indiana. We are truly sorry that we cannot be of more help.

"Nevertheless, having read your letter several times, I would like to assure you that any instructor who has inspired the kind of devotion that Redford O'Malley obviously has must be a very good one. I doubt that a mere certificate would have an impact on that. However, we have included a copy of our handbook for Mr. O'Malley. He can study this book should he ever have an interest in working at a camp or riding program in Indiana." Stevie refolded the letter with a flourish.

"You don't think he'd ever want to leave, do you?" Carole asked. They had all had such a good time with him while Max was in London that she felt even more appreciative of Red's skills. And he and Denise made a great teaching team.

Lisa shook her head. "He's not going to go anywhere fast. He's got Denise, his studies, a good job, and a boss who respects and trusts him. That should keep him right here in Virginia for a long time."

"Besides, if anything ever happens to Max, Red can take over," Stevie pointed out. "After all, he's practically married to Deborah!"

ABOUT THE AUTHOR

BONNIE BRYANT is the author of many books for young readers, including novelizations of movie hits such as *Teenage Mutant Ninja Turtles*® and *Honey, I Blew Up the Kid*, written under her married name, B. B. Hiller.

Ms. Bryant began writing The Saddle Club in 1986. Although she had done some riding before that, she intensified her studies then and found herself learning right along with her characters Stevie, Carole, and Lisa. She claims that they are all much better riders than she is.

Ms. Bryant was born and raised in New York City. She lives in Greenwich Village with her two sons.

THE SADDLE CLUB™

❑ 15594-6	HORSE CRAZY #1	$3.50/$4.50 Can.
❑ 15611-X	HORSE SHY #2	$3.25/$3.99 Can.
❑ 15626-8	HORSE SENSE #3	$3.50/$4.50 Can.
❑ 15637-3	HORSE POWER #4	$3.50/$4.50 Can.
❑ 15703-5	TRAIL MATES #5	$3.50/$4.50 Can.
❑ 15728-0	DUDE RANCH #6	$3.50/$4.50 Can.
❑ 15754-X	HORSE PLAY #7	$3.25/$3.99 Can.
❑ 15769-8	HORSE SHOW #8	$3.25/$3.99 Can.
❑ 15780-9	HOOF BEAT #9	$3.50/$4.50 Can.
❑ 15790-6	RIDING CAMP #10	$3.50/$4.50 Can.
❑ 15805-8	HORSE WISE #11	$3.25/$3.99 Can..
❑ 15821-X	RODEO RIDER #12	$3.50/$4.50 Can.
❑ 15832-5	STARLIGHT CHRISTMAS #13	$3.50/$4.50 Can.
❑ 15847-3	SEA HORSE #14	$3.50/$4.50 Can.
❑ 15862-7	TEAM PLAY #15	$3.50/$4.50 Can.
❑ 15882-1	HORSE GAMES #16	$3.25/$3.99 Can.
❑ 15937-2	HORSENAPPED #17	$3.50/$4.50 Can.
❑ 15928-3	PACK TRIP #18	$3.50/$4.50 Can.
❑ 15938-0	STAR RIDER #19	$3.50/$4.50 Can.
❑ 15907-0	SNOW RIDE #20	$3.50/$4.50 Can.
❑ 15983-6	RACEHORSE #21	$3.50/$4.50 Can.
❑ 15990-9	FOX HUNT #22	$3.50/$4.50 Can.
❑ 48025-1	HORSE TROUBLE #23	$3.50/$4.50 Can.
❑ 48067-7	GHOST RIDER #24	$3.50/$4.50 Can.
❑ 48072-3	SHOW HORSE #25	$3.50/$4.50 Can.
❑ 48073-1	BEACH RIDE #26	$3.50/$4.50 Can.
❑ 48074-X	BRIDLE PATH #27	$3.50/$4.50 Can.
❑ 48075-8	STABLE MANNERS #28	$3.50/$4.50 Can.
❑ 48076-6	RANCH HANDS #29	$3.50/$4.50 Can.
❑ 48077-4	AUTUMN TRAIL #30	$3.50/$4.50 Can.
❑ 48145-2	HAYRIDE #31	$3.50/$4.50 Can.
❑ 48146-0	CHOCOLATE HORSE #32	$3.50/$4.50 Can.
❑ 48147-9	HIGH HORSE #33	$3.50/$4.50 Can.
❑ 48148-7	HAY FEVER #34	$3.50/$4.50 Can.
❑ 48149-5	A SUMMER WITHOUT HORSES Super #1	$3.99/$4.99 Can.